BLACKBERRY WAY

Nobody knows the lanes and fields around Much Marlowes like forager Laura Ashcombe does. As autumn settles in, her kitchen is filled with tempting truffles and the heady perfume of quinces. Laura can go for days without seeing a soul — and that's just the way she likes it. Meanwhile, Stephen Henderson is finally beginning to get himself and his business back on track. And when his life collides with Laura's, it awakens in him something he's never felt before . . .

BLACKBERRY WAY

Nobody knows the lanes and fields around Much Ashcombe like forager Laura Ashcombe does. As autumn comes to her 'tribe' is filled with tumping trollies and the heady perfume of quinces. Laura can go for days without seeing a soul — and that's just the way she likes it. Meanwhile, Stephen Henderson is finally beginning to get himself and his business back on track. And when his life collides with Laura's, it awakens in him something he's never felt before . . .

EMMA DAVIES

BLACKBERRY WAY

Complete and Unabridged

LINFORD
Leicester

First published in Great Britain in 2017

First Linford Edition published 2022
by arrangement with
Bookouture
London

A catalogue record for this book is available
from the British Library.

ISBN 978–1–4448–4800–7

AUTUMN

1

From her vantage point just beyond the war memorial, Laura was able to watch Freya come and go with interest. Laura had seen her several times over the past few weeks and, at first, Freya had been completely oblivious of anyone's presence; but on a couple of occasions now, Laura had been caught unawares and Freya had seen her, giving her a beaming smile. She was only glad that today she had chosen to leave Boris behind. The dog had a habit of drawing attention, purely down to his enormous size, whereas Laura was tiny enough to lose herself behind a gravestone or in the shadow of a hedge. His absence gave Laura the opportunity to observe Freya unnoticed.

She'd only ever met Freya's father once or twice, but she knew the family — everyone did hereabouts — and a quick check of the headstone that Freya

3

visited had confirmed what she already knew. She didn't exactly remember him dying, but she had seen the freshly dug grave well over a year ago and had felt for Freya. Death was never an easy thing, especially for one so young and alone, and although Laura didn't know Freya at all, she knew of her, and in Laura's world that was generally enough. The family were well liked locally; they had a history and a tradition in the town which Laura approved of.

In all the time since his death, the grave had been well tended and yet she hadn't seen Freya in the churchyard until these last few weeks. People were creatures of habit and, as with most regular occurrences in their lives, like shopping, or going for a walk, visiting the grave of a loved one was most often undertaken on the same day or days and at roughly the same time. It was one of the things that made Laura feel safe; that way she knew what to expect. Something must have changed for Freya to alter her pattern of visits, and it wasn't until a few days ago when Laura had both arms plunged deep into a hedgerow, rooting out the juiciest blackberries that she realised how busy Freya must be with the apple harvest. Since then she had kept a wary eye.

* * *

Freya smiled as she pushed open the gate to the churchyard. The slanting early-morning sun had risen just high enough to touch the cobweb that hung from the lichen-covered wood and light up its dew-drop-covered strands like a diamond choker.

She took a deep breath in the damp air. She loved mornings like this when the mist swirled about her feet as she walked, knowing that in an hour or so it would lift to reveal a beautiful day, full of the colours she liked best. For now, the churchyard held a muted beauty and, as she made her way between the graves, she let her thoughts wander towards the coming day.

October was when the hard work really

began at Appleyard. The orchards had been quietly soaking up the sun and the rain all year, and now the apples were so ripe the trees were ready to offer them up like a gift; a reward for Freya's continued care and patience. Only this year had been different of course. This year her father no longer walked the rows of trees, but instead her beloved Sam. Her heart lifted at the thought that in a few short weeks she would be visiting this church again, but by the time she left, it would be as Sam's wife.

One short year ago, it had all been so different. She had come to the churchyard then, alone and frightened for her future, trying to cope with the all-consuming grief of losing her dad, and the threat of losing Appleyard, the house she had lived in all her life; her livelihood, and her stronghold. It had taken the wisdom of a curly-haired stranger to change all that, not only to bring Sam back to her, but life back to the orchards too. It was at about this time of year that Amos had arrived, walking up her drive to offer help with the harvest in return for food and a bed in her barn. He'd stayed until Christmas, until the wind had blown him on his way again, but there wasn't a day when Freya didn't long to see him one more time, to thank him for all that he had brought her.

She stopped in front of a small, neat headstone, tucked into the corner of the cemetery, and bent to her knees.

'Morning, Dad,' she said with a warm smile. 'And how are you this morning? It's going to be another beautiful day.'

She put down the bag she was carrying, her fingers automatically moving to collect the wilted blooms that filled the vases in front of the headstone. She lifted them to one side ready to dispose of. Then she rummaged in her bag for a pair of secateurs and began to gently clip away the faded heads of the bedding plants that she had planted in the late spring.

'I've brought you some Cyclamen today, Dad. I know you'll look after them much better than I can. I still can't manage to keep them alive, but I liked the colours.'

Freya's fingers were a little cold, but she worked quickly, keeping up a steady stream of chatter as she did so. Sometimes, she had the place to herself and sometimes not, but it never bothered her that others might be able to hear what she was saying. This was her time with her dad, and that was that.

'You should see the fields, Dad; they look amazing. I wouldn't be surprised if we don't start harvesting a couple of weeks early. The late burst of sunny weather we've been having is more than we could have wished for, and the juice presses are working overtime at the moment. That's why I've come so early today, so I hope you don't mind, but I've got to get back to give Sam a hand. Right, I'll be back in a minute.'

She gathered up the clippings and brown petals into a couple of sheets of newspaper and rose to take them to the small composting heap at the rear of the church. A trail of footprints through the dewy grass lay off to one side, and she followed their direction, trying to catch a glimpse of their owner.

Over the past few weeks as Freya's days had become busier, and her visits to her dad were earlier in the day, she had noticed another frequent visitor to the churchyard; a young woman, who looked much the same age as she, though tiny in stature. They had exchanged smiles on occasion, or at least Freya had, but they'd never spoken, and for some reason she intrigued Freya. It was her dog that Freya had noticed first: a huge Irish wolfhound that was almost as tall as the woman herself, and after that Freya found herself looking out for the slight figure with the beautiful heart-shaped face and huge almond eyes. She had an air of sadness about her, which was not all that unusual given the setting, but in all the times Freya had seen her, she had been in a different part of the churchyard, tending to a different grave, which was perhaps slightly odd. She lay flowers and wreaths, talking all the while just

9

like Freya did, but whether this was to herself or the occupants of the ground beneath her, Freya didn't know.

Today, apart from the footprints in the grass, Freya could see no sign of her, and placing her wilted flowers and clippings on the compost heap, she returned to finish her own tidying.

Ten minutes or so later, she was done. She couldn't stay too long; the day was going to be lengthy as it was, and the sooner she got back to Appleyard, the sooner she could give Sam a hand with the myriad tasks that needed attention.

'I'll be back on Sunday, Dad, so you make sure you keep out of trouble until then, won't you?'

She touched her fingers to her lips and placed them on top of the white marble headstone for a moment before getting to her feet.

'Bye Dad,' she called.

The sun was fully around the side of the church by the time Freya made her way back down the main path to the lane outside. It lit up the wet grass, setting it sparkling and she stopped for a moment to watch a robin whose beady eye was also on the ground, although for an entirely different reason. As she watched, it flew to perch on a gravestone for a second before swooping to the freshly turned earth in front of it. The little bird darted off again, a prize worm in its mouth, but not before something else had caught Freya's eye. Aside from the late flowering geraniums planted there, a beautiful wreath had been laid upon the grave, and Freya's feet moved towards it before she could stop herself.

She had spent the last few weeks endlessly searching through images on the internet and in wedding magazines for something which resembled the idea she had in her head; an idea which was refusing to go away until satisfied. None of the pictures she had seen had quite captured the look she was trying to achieve and, with their wedding at the end of the month, she was getting short on time. All the wedding flowers she'd seen were too ordered, too uniform; she wanted hers to be exuberant, a little unruly even, but above everything else, a celebration of the season and their harvest. The wreath lying in front of her was all these things and more, and Freya's heart began to beat a little faster. This was exactly what she had been looking for.

With a quick glance around her, she dropped to her knees, reaching out with tentative fingers to trace the outline of the leaves and to touch the vibrant berries and fruits; bright orange hips, the rosy red of crab apples, the deep purple damsons. Freya had never seen anything quite like it. It looked home-made and, although some of the leaves seemed to have been preserved in glycerine, the rest of the wreath looked as if it had been plucked from the hedgerow that morning. Her head darted up again, scanning the churchyard for any sign of life, but whoever had laid this wreath was long gone; Freya was on her own.

She checked her watch, grimacing at the time, and reluctantly stood up. She must get on with her day, but one thing was suddenly very clear in her mind; even if she had to stake out the church-yard, somehow, she would get to know the maker of this beautiful wreath, and she had just over three weeks to do it.

★ ★ ★

Laura liked having the churchyard to herself. This early in the morning there were rarely any other visitors, and those that had come, so far, had obeyed the unwritten rules of the churchyard. Grief was such a personal thing. It was private, unobtrusive. It swathed those suffering from it in a cloak of invisibility, made them unapproachable, even among their own kind. People didn't talk about death. Eyes remained downcast, conver-sations were muted, and voices kept low; this had always been Laura's experience, until Freya started coming to visit.

She had never got close enough to Freya to make out what she was say-ing, but she could see her lips moving and her arms waving, and she knew that during the whole time she visited her dad, the words never stopped. Nothing unusual about that as such; lots of people talked to their loved ones during visits, but what was rare was that Freya didn't seem to obey the unwritten rules. She laughed, she seemed to speak in a normal voice, her mouth was open and expressive, not closed and tightened as most people's were when they whispered or spoke softly, embarrassed. She spoke to her father as if he was standing next to her, even cocking her head to one side and listening for his reply. Freya greeted other people in the churchyard too, and not the scurrying polite head nod that most people achieved, but a broad, smiling greeting, and it unnerved Laura a great deal.

Today though, as Laura watched the young woman leave the churchyard, she had seen something else. Something that she recognised in herself, and which intrigued her even more. Freya had stopped by one of the wreaths Laura had made, and in that singular moment it was as if for Freya everything around her, save for the wreath, had paled from view. It was a sensation Laura often felt herself, particularly on a day like today when the colour of the landscape, or of a particular leaf transfixed her with wonder. Freya had reached out, almost holding her breath and the reverent look on her face echoed something deep within Laura. In a matter of moments Freya had gone, but she had left behind something that Laura hadn't felt in a long time, and a tiny, but nonetheless vital spark began to glow.

2

Laura was just about to pop another chocolate into her mouth when two hairy feet landed on the work surface beside her as Boris made his presence known. Reluctantly, she returned the chocolate to the tray in front of her, moving it swiftly out of the dog's reach. Despite the fact that they would do him no good at all, he seemed particularly attracted to these and, whenever she made them, would try every trick in the book to try to pinch one. So far, she had managed to evade his wily ways.

'Is that my shopping?' she queried the dog, with a glance at her watch as she moved out into the hallway. Sure enough she could see the outline of someone through the frosted half glass in her door. The figure was too tall to be her usual delivery driver, but she pulled open the door anyway.

A rather nervous-looking young man

stood there with a stack of plastic crates on a trolley.

Sometimes, Laura played a little game with them, when she was feeling in a particularly ruthless mood, but today had been a good one, so she smiled benevolently.

'Can you just pop them here?' she said, indicating a spot just beyond her door mat. 'That'll be fine.'

She gave Boris a stern command to sit while she ferried the bags back and forth to her kitchen, each time returning to give the delivery man a polite smile as he handed her more. When she had finished, she held out her hand to sign for the delivery and bade him a cheerful goodbye. He hadn't spoken once, but at least he hadn't shouted.

She realised her mistake as soon as she picked up the last bag. While it contained some breakfast cereal, a bottle of washing up liquid, a bag of rice and some lentils, it did not contain her two loaves of bread. Why on earth had she let the driver go without checking things first like she usually did? It didn't happen very often admittedly, but, on the few occasions that something had been missing from her order, it had always been discovered, still on the van, in a rogue bag that had somehow become separated from the rest. Now she would have to go and buy more. The making of a delicious leek and potato soup had also been on the day's agenda and she couldn't bear the thought of eating it without fresh bread.

Laura picked up a clean tea towel and draped it over the chocolates, snatching up one at the last minute and stuffing it into her mouth. She reached up to the hook on the back door and took down the dog lead that hung there.

'Come on, Boris,' she called. 'Walkies . . . again!'

It was just over a mile and a half into the village, so by the time she got back she would have lost most of the afternoon, but at least it meant she wouldn't have to go out again later in the day. A couple of new books had been delivered yesterday, and she was looking forward to an evening of reading. Taking this particular route into the village also meant that she could check to see how the sloes along the edge of the Williams' wood were coming along. By her reckoning, they should be pretty much perfect.

★ ★ ★

Stephen wasn't entirely sure he was enjoying exercise yet, but he had stuck at it, and it was getting easier. He was notching up several miles a day on his bike now, and even Long Lane hill didn't torture him quite as much any more. He was almost at the top now and looking forward to cresting the rise. On a day like today it was easy to see why people enjoyed cycling. The wind was almost non-existent; the air still warmed by the sun but with just enough bite to feel refreshing, and the view from the top of the hill would make everything worthwhile. The road sloped downwards, straight and true before disappearing around a sharp left-hand bend at the bottom. On one side, rich red earth stretched out in glistening furrows as far as he could see, and on the other, the deep blue of the sky was filled with majestic red, orange and yellow leaves from the trees that bordered the road.

He heard the car before he saw it, the engine roaring as it changed up into third and then fourth gear. He didn't think it was behind him, but as yet Stephen couldn't see where it was coming from. It was unusual enough to meet cars down this lane; it was narrow and there was a much quicker road away from the village that took most of the traffic, but the vehicles that did use it were never travelling this fast. His bike was building up speed as he travelled downhill, and he braked automatically, trying to retract his feet from the toe clips that held his feet fast on the pedals. One came loose almost immediately, but Stephen had always found the other much harder to disengage. He hadn't been riding for that long and didn't quite have the knack yet.

Something told him that he would need to stop soon, though, and pretty quickly, judging by the speed the car must be going. With his feet stuck in clips, there was only one possible outcome and Stephen knew from bitter experience that it would be painful.

He was still wrestling with his pedal when the car shot around the bend at the bottom of the road. By now, Stephen was almost halfway down the lane himself and as the car tore into the thick hedge at the side of the road, he could see that the driver had lost control and out of instinct yanked the steering wheel away from hedge, propelling the car onto the other side of the road and straight into his path. As he frantically tried to free his left foot, he leaned on his own brakes, making for the other side of the road. A flash of colour caught his eye as he swerved, an automatic yell leaving his lips in warning as, too late, he registered the slight figure in front of him calmly picking something from the bushes.

Laura felt a sudden hard shove as something made contact with the middle of her arm and she was pushed roughly to one side, spinning around so that she crashed through the bush, landing sprawled on her back. She was vaguely aware of something hurtling past her and, as she flailed her arms around to try and slow her downward movement, an even bigger shape shot past, only metres from where she lay. She stared at the road in shock, her heart pounding, a sharp stinging in her arm from the thorns which had torn at her skin as she fell. Within moments, a gentle wet nose poked at her as Boris came to her side, licking her face. She struggled into an upright position, chest still heaving, to see what had cannoned into her.

The cyclist was lying on his back too, his bike to one side, the front wheel buckled, the rear still spinning wildly. He'd obviously gone straight over the handlebars, and Laura flinched at the memory of doing this as a child. She got cautiously to her feet, but apart from the pain in her arm and a slight soreness in her backside, she was unhurt, more shocked than anything. She crept to the side of the prostrate figure, fervently hoping for no blood or broken bones, stopping dead when she saw him. She recognised his face instantly. Of all the people who could have crashed into her this afternoon, it would have to be Stephen bloody Henderson; arrogant pig. And what on earth was he wearing? She could feel the heat of her anger beginning to rise as she stood looking down at him. He might have really hurt her, careering about the countryside on a bike he clearly couldn't control properly. If he wanted to look like an over-stuffed sausage in that ridiculous Lycra get-up that was up to him, but she certainly didn't want to be involved in his midlife crisis.

She was about to walk away when both his eyes suddenly shot open and he lurched upwards, looking about him wildly, his breath coming in short pants. He struggled to focus, eventually homing in on her face as his brain seemed to catch up with the rest of him.

'Jesus, are you all right!' he exclaimed, trying to get to his feet. 'I could have killed you!'

Laura studied his face, unsure of what to say. In fact, she didn't want to say anything at all. Stephen's face was all screwed up, his jaw clenched. He certainly didn't look like he was sorry.

'I'm fine,' she stated, beginning to look around for the bag she had dropped. There was no way she was hanging around for a minute longer than necessary. She spied it caught up in the branch of one of the bushes, and was about to retrieve it when she felt an arm tugging at hers. She wheeled around.

'I said . . . what on earth were you doing just standing in the bushes like that? You're lucky I saw you at all.'

He was shouting now, his face contorted.

'I was picking sloes, not that it's any of

your business. What on earth were *you* doing riding that thing around when you clearly can't control it? And . . . if I'm not much mistaken, you were on the wrong side of the road.'

Stephen stared at her as if she had grown another head. 'Me? *I* was out of control? Didn't you see the bloody car going ninety miles an hour down the road? The one I swerved to avoid, the one that narrowly missed you? Are you blind or something?'

Laura bent down to retrieve her bag, picking up Boris' lead which was trailing on the ground. She turned back to Stephen and looked him squarely in the eye.

'No,' she said. 'I'm deaf.' And then she walked away.

3

Laura had only gone a matter of yards before she felt a sharp tug to her arm once more. Anger leaped into her throat. She turned swiftly.

'Will you stop grabbing my arm?' she snarled.

Stephen had the grace to step back slightly, looking momentarily abashed.

'And before you ask the bleeding obvious, I can lip-read, that's how. So, I can 'hear' what you said, but no I didn't hear the car tearing down the road, or you screeching across the road, or squealing your brakes or shouting, or any of those things that probably happened. Is that enough of an explanation for you, or do you need me to go on?'

Stephen stared at her. 'No, that's enough of an explanation,' he said, and she could see that he was no longer shouting. 'I had no idea, I'm sorry.'

'What? Sorry for hurling me into the

middle of a prickly bush or sorry because I'm deaf?'

There really was no answer to that, and Laura didn't expect one. She glared at Stephen for one last moment and then turned her back on him once more, stomping off down the lane. There was no tug to her arm this time.

* * *

Behind her, Stephen gazed after the slender figure, still trying to catch his breath. God, if she was this beautiful when she was angry, imagine what she would look like when she smiled.

* * *

Laura made it home in near record time. Even Boris, sliding in through the door after her, flopped onto his bed in the corner of the kitchen with a reproachful eye.

'And you can stop looking at me like that as well,' she muttered, fetching the dog a bowl of water.

She managed to fill the kettle, set it to boil, and place the teabag into her cup before the tears came. She had done it again. What on earth was the matter with her? She had never been like this before David died.

She prodded the tea bag viciously. She didn't really know what it was that made her act the way she did. Her walk had been lovely, the loaves she carried in her bag were fresh and fragrant, and she had enjoyed the balmy autumn air. On the face of it then she had been in a good mood, so why on earth had she felt the need to take Stephen apart the way she had? After all, despite the fact that she hadn't wanted to listen to what he had to say, it sounded as if he had come to her rescue in a roundabout way; even if that had necessitated shoving her to the ground. Her memory of the events leading up to their encounter was patchy, but Stephen hadn't fared too well himself. She could have offered some gratitude, or even a solicitous enquiry after his own health, but instead she had berated him for something which was obviously not his fault at all.

Anger seemed to come at her from nowhere these days, boiling up when she least expected it, and when it did, the resulting embarrassment only served to make her worse. Instead of apologising for her behaviour like any normal person, she cranked her abuse up a gear and then walked away; running back to the safety of her little cottage, to her warm kitchen, where she was alone and could ruminate on her shortcomings at length. Her anger scared her. Everything scared her, and today was another stark reminder of how vulnerable she was.

She took her tea to the table, wrapping her arms around Boris who had magically appeared at her side. The sloes were still in a bag by the sink where she had left them, but her impulse of earlier in the day had waned, and she couldn't be bothered to deal with them now. The dog's fur was warm and comforting, and it seemed easier simply to sit where she was for the time being and let herself be soothed.

It was some time before she moved again, reluctantly getting up to prepare the fruit. She made it a rule never to pick more than she needed, or to waste what she carried home. If nature had seen fit to provide such bountiful produce, then she was only allowed to pick, never plunder. This batch of sloes was destined for the freezer first, where it would sit for a couple of hours until covered with a layer of ice. So far, the autumn had been warm, and the first frosts of the year had yet to appear, so the sloes would benefit from their assisted freezing, releasing their juices and flavour into the alcohol she would steep them in much more readily as a result. It wasn't until she was running water into the sink to give the fruit a good wash that she remembered the connection between Stephen and Freya.

★ ★ ★

Stephen's journey home took much longer than Laura's. Although he too had anger to fire his pace, he was considerably further from home than she was, and his bike might as well be left to rust in the hedgerow for all the use it was now. Walking was not the simple option it first appeared to be either, given that the only footwear he had with him were his cycling shoes complete with cleats.

When she had first stomped off, Stephen had watched Laura's retreating back with a mixture of desire, shock, amusement and burning anger. He was reeling himself with the force at which he had been thrown from his bike, but whichever way he looked at it, he didn't think his responses to her had warranted the bitter words she had flung at him. His shoulder was aching badly, but as he watched her stalk away, getting smaller and smaller, he felt an odd emotion he hadn't experienced for quite some time: compassion. He would have run after her were it not for his shoes, and even though he knew he would probably be

31

attacked for his audacity; he had an over-whelming desire to explain, to soothe, to heal whatever had caused her to behave the way she had, and that wasn't like him at all.

He pulled his mobile from his pocket and peered at it closely; thankfully it seemed no worse for having had his bod-ily weight thrown upon it. He dialled his brother's number and waited for Sam to pick up. It rang for a while before it was answered.

'Hi Stephen.' Freya sounded breath-less. 'Were you after Sam, only he's a bit busy right now?'

Freya sounded like she was standing in the middle of football stadium. 'What on earth is all that noise?' asked Stephen.

He could hear Freya smile. 'Thirty-two school children, all getting high on apple juice,' she replied.

'What?' Stephen shouted.

'Miss Kennedy's class from the pri-mary school,' she explained. 'Year six have been tending the school garden this term, so they get to come and press the apples from their tree. You would never believe how exciting it is . . . I'd forgotten what it's like to be ten!'

Stephen groaned inwardly. He'd been banking on Sam effecting a swift rescue mission, but it sounded like they were up to their ears. He quickly explained his predicament.

'Stephen, that's awful! Did you see the car?'

'Not clearly. A dark blue four-by-four I think, which could fit the description of any number of cars around here. I was too busy trying not to get killed to take any more notice than that. And the driver was lucky he didn't end up wrapped around a tree, to be honest.'

'But it sounds as if you might have been. Are you sure you're okay?'

Stephen grimaced. 'I'll live,' he replied, circling his shoulder experimentally. 'Bit sore in places but nothing serious. Sadly, the same can't be said for my bike. I think the best course of action might be to put it out of its misery rather than let it suffer.'

Freya laughed. 'Well, at least you can still smile about it. Look if you can give me twenty minutes, I'll be there. Where exactly are you?'

* * *

Sitting on the verge to wait for Freya had been a serious mistake. Stephen was now so stiff he wasn't sure he could actually get up, and his shoulder throbbed painfully. He gave his bike a dirty look. This cycling lark was supposed to be a way of getting fit, not ending up feeling like he was a hundred and two. Perhaps some rigorous walking might suit him better, or even, if his knees could stand the strain, some gentle jogging. God forbid he should have to resort to sucking in his stomach in some fancy gym.

Stephen was still pondering the state of his girth, when Freya drew up. He levered himself off the ground through gritted teeth and hobbled over to join her.

'Do you want to chuck the bike in the

back?' she called.

Stephen looked back. 'Not really,' he said. 'Can't we just leave it there?'

Freya stepped down from the pickup. 'No, we can't,' she said. 'Go on, jump in, I'll sort it out. You might feel differently in the morning.' She gave him a big smile, but not before Stephen had seen her trying to stifle a giggle at the sight of him in Lycra. She didn't know quite where to look.

'So what exactly happened?' she asked, once the bike was stowed and they were on their way.

Stephen recounted the afternoon's events. 'I couldn't help it, Freya. She was standing right at the edge of the road, but I didn't spot her until I nearly mowed her down, she was almost completely hidden by the canopy of trees. What's worse is that I dread to think what might have happened if I hadn't shoved her out of the way. The car was travelling so fast, and fishtailing around the road, he could easily have taken her out, no problem at all.'

'And she was deaf, you said?'

Stephen nodded. 'Hmm, and beautiful.' He sighed. 'Possibly the most beautiful girl I've ever seen, but as first meetings go, it wasn't what you'd call auspicious. She let me know in no uncertain terms what she thought of me.'

'I bet she did,' said Freya, prodding hard at Stephen's arm with her free hand.

'Ow!' he protested. 'What was that for?'

'Just checking,' she replied. 'It would appear that you do have a soft spot after all.'

Stephen glared at her. 'Very funny,' he huffed. 'She could have been seriously hurt.'

Freya was instantly contrite. 'I know. I'm sorry, Stephen. I shouldn't take the mickey. You should probably go to the police you know.'

'And say what? I didn't see the car well enough to make an identification. I'm fine, our mystery girl is fine, and that's pretty much all there is to it.'

Freya thought for a minute. 'Yes, I

suppose. There ought to be something we can do, though. It doesn't seem right that something so potentially serious is just ignored.'

Stephen stared through the windscreen at the road ahead, lost in his own thoughts for a moment. When he eventually answered, his voice had a soft almost wistful tone to it. 'Well, there is one thing I'm going to do,' he said. 'And that's find her . . . whoever she is.'

4

Laura was up early the next morning.
She had checked her diary before she
went to bed the previous evening and
would have to be out early if she was to
get all her deliveries made before she
visited the churchyard. In the dark days
immediately after David's death, her
neighbours, Stan, Millie and Blanche
had been her lifeline. They were just as
cantankerous as she was in many ways
and her grief-stricken protestations that
she didn't need to eat or drink had fallen
on deaf ears. She had been practically
force-fed chicken soup, beef stew and
shepherd's pie, and although Laura had
fought them almost every step of the
way, in the end she had been grateful for
their kindly ministrations and their present arrangements had grown from there.

All three of her neighbours were some-
where between the ages of sixty-five and
eighty, with Blanche, Laura suspected,

being the eldest. She had never liked to ask their ages, as all three were fiercely independent and as sprightly as someone half their age and, unlikely though the friendships were, they were firm.

Stan lived the closest to her, although still a good half mile away; a keen vegetable grower with a very sweet tooth and an intense fondness for her chocolate-coated boozy damsons. Three doors down from him was where Millie lived. She was the youngest of the trio and a stalwart member of the WI. Her cakes were to die for, although alas her jam was not, and so in return for her sweet treats, Laura left Millie with plain labelled jars of apple and ginger or raspberry jam. So what if on occasion she passed them off as her own; Millie's secrets were safe with her. Blanche lived in the next house, with her motley collection of chickens that had all been rescued from some place or another. With Blanche's tender care, they laid the biggest eggs Laura had ever seen, and as Blanche liked nothing more than a drop of sloe gin each evening, purely for medicinal purposes of course, the trade was a steady one.

Laura was well aware that these arrangements allowed her to stay outside the real world for much of the time, but she was also able to keep a watchful eye over her friends and, in an age that often felt unkind and uncaring to Laura, it helped to assuage her guilt over the darker aspects of her own character. Hiding from the world was not the answer of course, but life was certainly much easier this way.

It took Laura nearly an hour-and-a-half to make the round trip this morning despite the fact that Blanche wasn't in. Her friends were early risers like her, and it was nice to share a cup of tea with them, talking about their plans for the day and their love of the coming season. She returned home laden with runner beans, some courgettes, and a honey cake. With her bounty deposited safely in the kitchen, Laura was finally ready to set out for the churchyard. She slipped down the path to one of the sheds at the end of her garden to collect her tools and a garland she had made a couple of days earlier. The conkers in it were gleaming like newly polished mahogany, and she smiled to see them. Mr and Mrs Roberts were going to love them too.

* * *

'Morning, Dad,' called Freya. 'I hope you don't mind me visiting two days in a row, although actually . . .' she lowered her voice to a whisper, '. . . it isn't you I've come to see at all, sorry.'

She perched on the little stool she had brought with her for the days when the grave didn't need tending and she just wanted to sit and chat.

'Sam thinks I'm barmy of course, but then, no offence Dad, he's a bloke, so what does he know? To be fair, he's been pretty good with all the other wedding arrangements, but you know him as well as I do, and he hasn't got a creative bone in his body, has he? I know exactly how I want my bouquet and the other arrangements to look and, as I was leaving here yesterday, I saw the most beautiful wreath.' She sighed, looking around her once more. 'Even though it pains me to say it, it was much better than anything I could make, and I know that whoever did would be the perfect person to help with the wedding. Unfortunately, I don't know who that is.'

She cocked her head to one side as if listening. 'So you need to help me out here, Dad, because I'm pretty much lying in wait to see if I can spot whoever made the wreath, and if you don't talk to me, I'm going to look a complete loon.' She gave a wry smile. 'Yeah, I know. Thanks for the obvious witty response.' Her head whipped around as she heard the lychgate creak open, but it was only the wind; she probably hadn't fastened it properly.

A tiny robin swooped in front of her, a small worm in its mouth, and she followed the path of its flight, watching as it disappeared behind a rather ornate memorial at the far end of the churchyard. She smiled, turning back to speak to her father once more, before looking up again to where the robin had flown. I *wonder*, she thought.

'Excuse me for a minute, Dad.'

Freya had done a circuit of the grave-yard as soon as she had entered it this morning, but there had been no one else there, and she had wandered among the graves looking for more evidence of the wreath-maker's work. It was a large cemetery, with a newer area off to the right of the church, where Freya's dad was buried, and with the original, older graves dotted around the rear of the church and along a low boundary wall to the left. At the far end of the wall however, an arch led through into a separate much older space where there were larger memorials and family plots; even a small crypt for one of the most notable village families. It was obvious that some of these plots were still being well cared for, and even though Freya had not seen any other wreaths, it set her thinking.

Since her arrival she had seen no one

else enter the churchyard, even though her view of the gate from her father's grave was uninterrupted. Now she wondered whether anyone would come into the grounds from the footpath through the fields that ran alongside this older area. There was still an old stile at one end and, although it was now partially hidden in the yew hedge, it was possible that people still used it. After all, robins were known for being friendly little birds, especially if the person they were keeping company was digging . . .

She followed the tiny bird as it darted to and fro between two of the larger memorials, and immediately she could see the source of the robin's excitement. Between two of the graves a triangular flower bed had been freshly dug and planted with winter flowering pansies. A small fork and trowel lay close by, along with a green canvas bag. Of their owner she could see no trace, but as Freya grew closer, a gentle voice floated up from behind one of the headstones.

'Hello, little one,' it said.

Freya smiled, knowing instantly who the voice was talking to. It was exactly how she addressed robins herself whenever they perched close by. Judging by the tilt of their heads, they always seemed to know they were being spoken to, and she loved the gleam in their intelligent black eyes.

She moved forward a little hesitantly. Freya didn't hold with whispers and tiptoes in the graveyard; to her, the place was as much about the living as the dead, but she did respect other people's need for privacy. She didn't want to blunder into someone's precious time with a relative, but neither did she want to creep up on them without announcing her presence. Of course, the person behind the gravestone might well not be the one she was looking for, and then a rather awkward conversation would ensue.

Freya sauntered past the flower bed, stopping to look at it in admiration before moving beyond the grave and on towards the memorials as if she wanted to study their inscriptions. As she turned, she was now able to see the figure who had previously been hidden from view. Her back was towards her, but Freya instantly recognised the woman she had seen here before. She was tending the grave, arranging the stems of some bright orange and purple dahlias in a vase, and at her side lay the most beautiful foliage wreath.

Freya cleared her throat, but there was no response. Instead, the woman began to speak herself.

'There you are now, Mrs Roberts. Didn't I tell you he would bring you your favourite flowers next time? The most beautiful colours they are too. A deep burnt orange and purple the exact same colour as a red cabbage.' She paused for a moment to adjust a stem. 'He's definitely a keeper,' she said. 'Any man who goes to the trouble of finding you your favourite flowers is worth hanging on to I reckon. What do you say?'

The flowers were certainly beautiful, and Freya smiled at the words. They were just the sort of daft thing she would say to her dad. The voice continued.

'And you look absolutely beautiful, Ethel, doesn't she Ted? That must be the prettiest dress I've ever seen. Brings out the colour of your eyes too. Speaking of which . . .' She reached down to lift up the wreath from beside her. 'I made this for you. After all it's not every day you get to celebrate an anniversary, is it? I hope you like it.'

Freya couldn't help herself. 'I think it's perfect,' she said, realising too late that she had intruded into a private conversation. She expected to receive a withering glare, but the woman moved only to lay the wreath in front of the headstone.

'Now you two have the most magical day, won't you?' she said, as she began to rise. 'And remember . . . don't do anything I wouldn't do!'

The smile was still on her lips as she stood and turned, dying the instant she saw Freya. A hand rose to her chest.

'Oh my God, you made me jump!'

Her sudden surprise jolted Freya too, and she put out a hand towards the woman as if to steady them both. 'I'm sorry,' she said swiftly. 'Really. I didn't mean to.'

The young woman gave a wary smile. 'It's okay, no permanent harm done.' She regarded Freya curiously with narrowed eyes. 'Were you talking to me just now? I'm sorry, I didn't hear you.'

'Well, I was very rude, butting into your conversation like that, so it's as well you didn't.'

The woman looked confused. 'My conversation? Oh, with Mr & Mrs Roberts.' She swung around to face the grave once more. 'Bless them. It's their wedding anniversary today — eighty-six years, would you believe it?' She gave Freya a quick smile. 'Actually,' she said, 'I don't know them at all; theirs is just one of the graves I'm paid to look after, so for all I know, they hated one another's guts, but I like to dream, you know . . .'

There it was again, thought Freya, the wistful sadness that she had glimpsed on her face before, in those huge brown eyes.

'I think it's lovely, the way you talk to them. I do the same with my dad whenever I visit. One of these days I swear he'll tell me to shut up, but for now I just chatter away. That way I feel like he's still with me somehow, if that makes any sense.'

'It makes perfect sense,' said the woman. 'I've seen you I think, haven't I? On the other side of the church,' she said shyly.

Freya nodded. 'My dad died in April last year,' she replied, dropping her head. 'Although some days it feels like it was yesterday.'

Silence stretched out for a moment before Freya looked back up again to find the woman staring at her. She smiled. 'I'm Freya, by the way.'

There was a slightly puzzled frown. 'Freya?' she repeated, looking for an answering nod. 'Okay. Well, I'm Laura.'

The two women looked warily at one another, Freya feeling a little embarrassed until she remembered what she had wanted in the first place. She coughed a little self-consciously.

'I hope you don't mind me asking, but is it you who makes the beautiful wreaths I've seen? The one just there, and another over by the lychgate; I noticed it yesterday.'

'Oh, the garlands?' Laura blushed. 'The hedgerows are bursting with such lovely stuff at the moment, it seems a shame not to share it.' She looked around her. 'It's nice to use flowers and plants on the graves, but the garlands are a little bit different.'

'I think they're absolutely beautiful,' said Freya. 'In fact, they're the nicest I've ever seen.'

'Thank you.' Laura blushed again, tipping her head to acknowledge the compliment. 'I enjoy making them, that's all.'

Freya could feel her excitement of yesterday beginning to return. 'Do you make other things as well, arrangements I mean, or is it just the garlands?'

She was dismayed to see Laura's face close up a little.

'Not really,' she said. 'I just fiddle with things, when I see something that I like, but they're just for me . . . or for my friends here.' She indicated the grave behind her.

It was a funny choice of words, thought Freya, noting that Laura's hands were now clasped around her elbows as if she was cold. She decided to back off a little.

'I make wreaths too, at Christmas time,' Freya said. 'But they're far more traditional than yours. I can't always find the things I want, or enough of them at any rate. I sell them you see, at the Mistletoe Fair in Tenbury Wells, but they have to be pretty uniform, so I need plenty of raw materials. I've used fruits and berries in the past, crab apples too, but I don't really have the time to seek them all out any more.'

'You have the orchard, don't you?' cut in Laura. 'Out on the Witley road.'

Her question surprised Freya. 'Yes,' she began tentatively, 'Appleyard. Do you know it?' she asked.

Laura bit her lip. 'I know of it,' she

said eventually. 'There's a place about three fields over where you can find crab apples, or huge orange haws. They're usually still about, even at Christmas.'

Freya smiled. 'Maybe you could tell me more one day.' She gave a quick glance at her watch. 'I have to get going in a minute, but I expect I'll see you here another time.'

'I'm here most days,' replied Laura quietly. 'Except at the weekend. I never come then, it's too . . . busy,' she said. She crossed to pick up her bag and tools. 'I should be off as well.'

Freya had to say something now or she had the feeling that the right time would never present itself. She gave a nervous smile.

'Laura, I hope you don't mind me saying . . . well, asking really, but I didn't come here by chance this morning; I came to see you.' She continued quickly at the sight of Laura's horrified face. 'Only because I meant what I said — I do absolutely love your garlands, but also because I've been looking for someone who could make things like this for a while now. I'm getting married soon, and these would be perfect for the wedding. They'd tell our story so beautifully...' She trailed off, unsure how to frame her question without it sounding too scary. In the end, she decided to simply spit it out. 'Would you consider helping me with our wedding flowers...? It's in three weeks.'

Laura's expression was unchanged.

'Look, you don't have to give me an answer now. It's a lot to ask, and I know I'm a bit of a bull in a china shop sometimes, but will you think about it at least? I'd pay you of course, and we could talk about it...'

Laura held her look for a moment, and Freya could see the turmoil reflected in her face. She was glancing about her as if checking she had everything she had brought with her, swapping the bag into her other hand.

'I'll think about it,' said Laura. 'But I'm not very good with people since...' She stopped abruptly. 'I'll think it about it,' she repeated, with the ghost of a smile. 'Thank you.' And she turned to go.

Freya watched her making her way to the stile and back to the fields. 'It was nice to meet you,' she called after Laura's retreating back; but there was no reply.

It wasn't until she had said goodbye to her dad and collected her stool that the penny dropped. It suddenly came to her why Laura hadn't appeared to hear her at times, why she wore a slightly intense expression whenever Freya was speaking, how she studied her face, and how her replies were not as quick as they might have been. She was lip-reading. Laura was deaf.

Freya thought of the last conversation she'd had with her future brother-in-law. Now what were the chances of that?

5

Stephen had apples to harvest, he shouldn't still be sitting in his kitchen, but unaccountably he couldn't move from his laptop. He had never felt this way before, but now that he did, he was revelling in the experience. He was also beginning to realise that if this was how he felt, then this 'thing', which he had hitherto believed to be a made-up, or certainly overrated, emotion must be true. It suddenly made him understand people a whole lot better.

Take his brother for example. Sam had been head over heels in love with Freya since the minute they clapped eyes on one another at primary school. Of course, back then, Sam hadn't recognised what love was; he and Freya were simply good friends until his hormones kicked in, and Freya's too for that matter. Stephen had watched them over the years, from his vantage point of superior age, and thought them soppy and foolish with their plans and declarations. It hadn't stopped him feeling jealous, though, of the affection that Sam received, and of the easy relationship he shared with a woman instead of the furtive fumblings that Stephen managed. And because he couldn't understand it, because he could never have it, he set out to take what was not rightfully his.

He had wooed Freya and seduced her with make-believe affection and lies; promises he never intended to keep. Everything bigger and better than his brother could ever hope to give her. She had fallen for it too, right up to the point where they were about to walk down the aisle, Sam long since fallen by the way-side. But something had made Freya stop, and when she stopped, she started running.

It had taken a very long time, right up until a year ago in fact for Stephen to be forgiven, and for Freya and Sam to finally get back to where they were always meant to be: together. Stephen had begun to acknowledge a different way of living since then. He'd had a great many lessons to learn, but slowly he was beginning to understand that things happened to other people not because they were favoured, or lucky, but because they worked for them. He realised, in fact, just how much of a prat he'd been in his life, giving in to jealousy and sullen, petty anger when he should have been forging his own future. For much of it, his had been a wasted life, but Stephen was determined to do better from now on, and two days ago, he had come across the most perfect, and most beautiful incentive.

It wasn't a very promising start, Stephen would be the first to admit, but really, if you looked at it from a slightly different point of view, he had saved the woman's life. Perhaps, in time, she would see it that way too, and they would laugh about how they had both behaved badly, saying things they hadn't meant, jumping to the wrong conclusions. There was no possibility that Stephen could have known she was deaf, but now that he did, he was determined to make up for it. He just needed a way to impress her somehow. That and hope that fate would allow them to meet up again, and she would stay in the same room with him for long enough to make it count.

He opened a new internet tab on his laptop and typed 'British Sign Language courses' into the search engine. So far that morning he had watched about thirty YouTube clips, searching for some simple words or phrases that might be relatively easy to learn. Even just 'hello' or 'thank you' would be a start, anything that might let her know that he wasn't a hot-headed idiot all the time . . .

★ ★ ★

'I should never have gone,' said Freya, as she and Sam sipped a welcome cup of tea. They'd been hard at it since early morning, but several hours' work had resulted in an enormous pile of perfect apples, ready for pressing. The afternoon, if they were lucky, would see the bright crisp juice, bottled and ready to be collected.

'It was a rotten thing to come out with when I didn't even know the girl. She must have been petrified having me throw that at her.'

Sam looked at Freya over the rim of his mug. 'And did she seem petrified?'

'Not exactly, but she didn't seem that happy either. She was obviously really shy, and now I know why. I'd never have asked her if I'd known.'

'Why would her being deaf make any difference?'

'Well because . . . imagine how she must feel?'

'Chuffed to know how much you liked her work?'

Freya gave an exasperated tut. 'Honestly, Sam. I was obviously making her very uncomfortable. I mean, she spends her days talking to dead people for God's sake, probably so that she doesn't have to hold embarrassing conversations with complete strangers who don't know a thing about her, and yet make wild suggestions at the drop of a hat.'

Sam merely smiled. 'Or,' he said pointedly, 'she could be very lonely but unsure about how to make things any different. It must be quite isolating being deaf; think about that for a minute. And now here you are, the first person in ages who's taken any notice of her, and not only that but showered her with compliments, and made her what could be a very exciting offer. Have you thought of it that way?'

He took hold of her hand. 'I'm wondering who's the more embarrassed here, Freya; are you sure it's Laura? Don't treat her any differently just because she's deaf, that's possibly the real reason she shies away from people; because she's so fed up with people treating her that way.'

Freya sighed. 'How did you get to be so wise, Sam Henderson?'

'Probably because I'm getting married to you, Freya Sherbourne. Isn't that why we're having this conversation? To convince you of something you already know is true. Don't give up on her, Freya, maybe she needs you more than you know.'

'But she didn't come to the church-yard today.'

'Perhaps she was busy. You could always try again tomorrow.'

Freya flashed him a huge smile before leaning over and kissing him deeply. 'I love you,' she said.

★ ★ ★

Two miles away Laura was having the exact same argument with herself, and with Boris when he could be bothered to listen. The dog's head was resting on the table as he sat beside it, his eyes swivelling to the left and then the right as he watched Laura pacing back and forth across the kitchen.

'I should be thrilled that someone likes my garlands so much and, more than that, she's even offered me paid work — for a wedding of all things! Do

61

you know what this could mean for me, Boris? Money. Money to help me get other things off the ground instead of sitting in my kitchen wasting my life away like the sad, lonely widow I am.'

She stopped pacing for a moment to look the dog squarely in the eye.

'I shouldn't even be having this conversation with you. I mean, it's obvious what the answer is. I should run after her as fast as I can and bite her arm off. But instead I'm having a deep and meaningful conversation with my dog because I'm scared, and pathetic and frightened that as soon as I'm among people again, they'll start saying all those horrible things about me that put me here in the first place.'

The memories of that time leaped out at her unbidden. It was a time and place that Laura never wanted to go back to, but even as her eyes began to smart with the pain of it all, a part of her knew that she had to go back to start going forward again.

'See, it's different with the others, my

friends; they're outcasts like me, because their age makes them different, makes them less able. But they're patient, they speak slower, and it's not half so exhausting having a conversation with them. Besides, Blanche is pretty deaf too, Stan has a dodgy hip and Millie's memory isn't what it once was; but none of us needs to apologise. We all know what it's like to have bits of us that don't work properly, and that's okay. We're still us.'

She sat down heavily with a sigh.

'I might not get a chance like this again. There was something . . . something I can't explain about Freya, but it's like she understood me. She wouldn't think it weird that I tramp the fields all day and forage for stuff. *She'd* think it was magical; she'd want to do it too, I know she would. No one has made me feel like that about what I do in a long time, Boris, a very long time indeed.' She puffed out her cheeks. 'And yet I still bloody chickened out.'

She got up again and walked over to her larder returning with a large bowl of pale knobbly fruits.

'Right,' she said in a decisive fashion. 'Tomorrow I'll go. Did you hear that, Boris?' The dog watched her with his large brown eyes, licking his lips as he did so. 'Tomorrow I *will* go to the church-yard, and I will meet with Freya and find out what it is she'd like me to do. So, if I look like I'm chickening out, I give you full permission to push me out through the door with a very wet cold nose.'

She gave a satisfied nod.

'And now that's decided, I'm going to tackle these beautiful quinces. Stick your nose in there, Boris, aren't they some of the best things you've ever smelled?'

6

Freya's heart leaped as she walked through the church gate the next morning. Laura was waiting for her on the other side, her huge dog beside her, and although she looked pretty terrified, Freya acknowledged that she'd found her own legs a little wobbly at times as she walked up the lane.

Two days ago, she had chatted away to Laura the same way she would to anyone else, but although she knew that today ought to be no different, she felt clumsy and tongue-tied. *Whatever you do, don't try and compensate for her deafness by shouting at her* was Sam's less than helpful advice. She had worked that out herself, but she still felt she ought to try to make things easier for Laura, she just didn't know how. The more she thought about their encounter, the more she could see her old friend serendipity at work. The fact that Stephen had quite literally bumped into Laura as well, only served to strengthen her feelings.

She gave Laura a tentative but she hoped friendly smile. The last thing she wanted to do was scare her off.

To her surprise, Laura responded with a massive grin of her own.

'Thank God, you're here,' she said. 'It took me all of yesterday to work up the courage to come. If you hadn't turned up, I would have felt the most enormous prat. I'd probably have gone home and had the most almighty blub as well.'

'Me too,' replied Freya. 'I'm so glad you came.'

The two women looked at one another for a moment, the early morning sun slanting a band of gold between them. It would be all right, thought Freya, and her nervousness faded.

'Well, this is Boris,' said Laura, patting the dog's head, which came easily to her waist. 'He's very big and very hairy, but other than that the least scary dog I know. In fact, he's a real pushover, but don't tell him I said that.'

Freya smiled at the hairy beast. 'It suits him,' she said. 'Very distinguished.'

When there was no reply, Freya lifted her head a fraction to find Laura squinting at her. She blushed.

'I said his name suits him.' She smiled. 'He looks very distinguished.'

There was a nod and then, 'I'm sorry, I . . .'

'Distinguished?' Freya repeated, trying not to shout.

'Ah, okay,' said Laura, 'I've always thought so. There's definitely something of the aristocrat about him.' She flashed Freya a grateful look before looking down and fiddling with the buttons on her coat.

'Perhaps I should just come out and say it . . .' began Laura. 'It might save us both a lot of embarrassment, and I can see you've worked out for yourself that I'm deaf. I probably should thank you first for not shouting. You won't believe how many people do, it's instinctive I know, but people's faces and mouths contort when they do that, and it makes lip-reading so much harder. Speaking normally is best.'

'I'll probably get it wrong a lot of the time, but I won't mind in the slightest if you tell me.'

'You might, when it's the nineteenth time I've done it,' said Laura with a wry smile.

Her words were light, but it struck Freya how utterly exhausting it must be for her to have a conversation this way, having to prompt people constantly to repeat things, having to study people's faces to such an extent that you see every flicker of irritation written there.

'How long have you been deaf?' she asked.

'Since I was about eighteen,' replied Laura. 'I had a brain tumour ... everything's fine now,' she hastened to add. 'Luckily for me, it wasn't particularly nasty, it just decided to grow in a rather unfortunate place, that's all. Come to think of it when you have a brain tumour, pretty much everywhere is unfortunate, but when it grew large enough to operate on, it had to come out. There was a substantial risk to my hearing, but a risk I had to take if I was to keep my other faculties.'

'The lesser of many evils. Not a huge comfort I would imagine.'

'It could have been worse,' said Laura.

Freya nodded sadly. 'I suppose,' she agreed. 'And would you normally sign . . . ? If you had the choice, I mean.'

Laura smiled. 'Yes,' she said, her hands flashing in front of her. 'It's a lot easier . . . for me anyway.'

'Maybe you could teach me,' said Freya, wincing as the words came out of her mouth. 'Or maybe I should just shut up and tell you about our wedding plans and what I had in mind for the flowers, and we can take it from there? I've brought one or two pictures I can show you too.' She shot Laura an apologetic look and was pleased to see she looked a little relieved. One thing at a time, Freya reminded herself, one thing at a time.

'We could go inside if you like,' said Laura. 'There's a small room at the side of the church with a table and chairs, and you could show me what you've brought.'

Freya followed Laura who led the way to a small anteroom just off the main entrance. Boris loped in by her side and immediately made for the only rug in the room beneath the small oak table. She gave a little shiver which had nothing to do with the coolness of the building, but instead to a flowering of nerves in the pit of her stomach. She would be here in three short weeks, walking through the huge oak door as a bride and leaving an hour later as Sam's wife. Between now and then there was an extraordinary number of things to attend to, and even though it wasn't a big wedding, Freya wasn't sure how on earth she would manage to pull it all off. If Laura would agree to help her, it would be a huge weight off her mind.

She sat down, waiting for Laura to follow suit before fishing in her bag for the photos she had brought.

'These aren't really right, but it's the

colours I like and the general look I'm aiming for.' She straightened up, placing the pictures down on the table.

Laura sat looking at them, an expectant look on her face. It was only when a lengthening silence began to stretch out that Freya realised her mistake. She gently touched a hand to Laura's arm.

'I'm sorry,' she said, once Laura's eyes were on her face. 'I was talking at the same time as bending down. I forgot you wouldn't hear me.'

Laura looked back at the pictures. 'People have a tendency to talk to the thing they're discussing, rather than each other. Tap the table or my arm when you're going to speak, that way I know to look at you.' She smiled. 'I like these, though, except they're a bit too regimented for my taste. Too confined. I like my arrangements to be more unstructured, messy even sometimes . . .' She frowned. 'Sorry, what was it you said?'

'The same as you,' answered Freya, feeling excited at the connection between them. 'I like the colours of these, but they're way too formal.'

Laura nodded. 'And what are we talking about here, in terms of decoration I mean. What do you need help with? The church, your own flowers?'

Freya screwed up her face. 'Erm . . . everything. The church yes, and my bouquet, but we're having a marquee back at Appleyard for the reception as well, and I'd love to have flowers there too. In fact, not just flowers, but fruits, leaves, berries, that kind of thing.'

At the mention of the marquee, Laura's eyes widened. She looked shocked, and yet Freya didn't think it was extravagant, not by modern standards.

'It won't be huge, the marquee I mean. It's just that we've nowhere else to put people. The barn is full of equipment, and —'

'How many people will there be?' interrupted Laura. She blanched suddenly, shooting backwards in her chair. Her hand flew to her mouth. 'I'm sorry, Freya. I can't do this. I shouldn't have come.'

Laura was almost at the door by the time Freya had registered her sudden change of mood. She struggled to get up, hampered by the straps of her bag which had become tangled in the chair leg.

'Laura, wait!' she shouted, without thinking. She looked beseechingly at Boris who looked rather startled at the sudden movement. 'Can't you stop her?' she asked. There was nothing for it but to chase after her. God, Laura was fast.

She was halfway down the path before Freya caught up with her, catching at her arm as gently as she could. She turned Laura to face her and was horrified to see that tears had already stained her pale face.

'Whatever is the matter?' she asked. 'I'm sorry, I didn't mean to upset you.'

Laura stared at her as if unseeing.

'It's my fault. I should never have come,' she hiccupped. 'All the villagers, all those people . . .'

Freya was confused now. 'What people? Who are you talking about, Laura?'

Laura's eyes searched her face for

answers. 'In the marquee, and at the church. Everywhere. I can't be with those people,' she said, shuddering.

It wasn't so much what she said but the way she said it which struck a chord with Freya. Being shy was one thing, but this was something entirely different. She recalled Laura's words of a couple of days ago. How she wouldn't visit the churchyard at the weekend because there were too many people, how she wasn't very good with folk since . . . a sentence that had never been finished. Freya could understand Laura feeling awkward in company. Deafness was not visible on the outside, and her life must be full of misunderstandings and apologies, judgements made, often incorrectly, as people mistook Laura's silence or lack of response for rudeness. But feeling awkward, although understandable, was not the issue here; it went much deeper than that. Laura was afraid.

Without thinking Freya reached out and pulled Laura in towards her, wrapping her arms around the tiny figure but saying nothing. It was an instinctive gesture, and Freya, not prone as yet to maternal feelings, was surprised by it; but there was something about Laura that was so gentle, so vulnerable, and although they were of a similar age, it touched something deep inside Freya. At first, she thought she had made a massive error as Laura's whole body went taut, but almost immediately she inhaled a huge shuddering breath and her arms clung to Freya's coat as she fell against her.

A cold wet nose pushed itself onto the back of Freya's hand several minutes later, as Boris reminded her gently of his presence. He seemed as confused about his mistress's behaviour as she was, but Laura's choice of a dog known for its loyalty and generosity was no coincidence. She wondered how long it had been since Laura had felt the reassurance of a human touch.

After a few moments more, Freya gently moved away, pulling Laura so that she could look at her. She had shed the tears she needed to, but her look when she met Freya's gaze was still fearful.

'Perhaps you should come and tell me all about it,' said Freya. 'If you're ready?'

There was a weak smile, but Laura was indeed ready. She had waited a very long time to talk to someone.

★ ★ ★

'We used to live next door to one another, had done ever since I was five and he was six, and I guess we grew up together. It wasn't until we started secondary school that I really took any notice of him; David was simply always there. It was never serious; we went out together a few times, but that all changed when I was fourteen and diagnosed with a brain tumour.'

Freya was beginning to feel cold, and the hard, wooden chair wasn't helping, but she sat as still as she could for fear of breaking the moment. Laura had begun to talk the moment they were back inside the church again, sitting in the same room they had left only minutes earlier. She nodded encouragingly.

'It's at those times that you find out who your friends really are,' she continued. 'I remember clearly the day when I told my best friend, Chloe, the diagnosis. I'd been in and out of hospital for weeks having various tests, and missed a fair bit of school one way or another. Chloe was brilliant. Every day I was absent, she came around to our house to fill me in with all the gossip, or help me to catch up with my homework; but the very day I was finally able to confide in her the diagnosis, she looked at me and said 'So, you're going to die then?'

The spot on the wall held Laura's attention for so long that Freya was tempted to look there herself, but eventually the words started again, a quiet monotone that belied Laura's true feelings.

'She apologised straight away of course, but I'd caught her off guard, and she'd said the first thing that had come into her head — the thing she really thought. It was what she believed, and

77

at the time, so did I.' She took another breath. 'It certainly spelled the death sentence for our friendship. She didn't walk away immediately, just sort of drifted further off each day, like a piece of flotsam caught on the outgoing tide, until I hardly saw her. And I let her go. I was too preoccupied to care, and where she and others left little holes in my life, David came and filled them.'

For the first time since she started talking, Laura raised her eyes and looked at Freya. The loneliness in her eyes was stark, as was the longing for warmth and life.

'I'm so sorry,' whispered Freya. 'That must have been an awful time for you. I can't imagine how you must have felt. School and just being fourteen are hard enough to get through, but add something like that into the mix . . . How ever did you cope?'

There was a slight pause as Laura weighed up what Freya had just asked.

'Strangely enough, it got easier after that. It was just David and me against the world. We didn't need anyone else. That's where I went wrong of course, but at the time I didn't think beyond the next day and the day after that; everything else was too far in the distance, and so it went on. Even when I found out about the operation and the risk to my hearing, David simply said we would learn sign language together, and so we did. It never crossed my mind that this was wrong . . .'

'What do you mean wrong, Laura? I'm not sure I follow you.' Freya put out a hand in reassurance.

It took Laura some moments before she could speak again, a sudden welling up of tears tightening her throat, and quickening her breathing. 'Because now that he's gone, I have nothing in my life, and no one. I built my world around him, and when he died, my foundations went too, and everything crumbled around me.'

Freya took in a sharp breath at the shock of Laura's words. Here she was, on the threshold of sharing a life with the man she loved, and this young woman had already lived a lifetime of love and grief. She was flooded with remorse. She left her chair and knelt beside Laura, taking both of her hands and folding them in her own. They were like ice.

'I'm so, so, sorry,' she said, making sure that Laura could see every word. 'I've been gabbling on about my own wedding without a second thought, and I never even stopped to think. I feel awful asking for your help, it was probably the most insensitive thing I could have done.'

'And yet I want to help,' whispered Laura, 'I just don't know how.'

Freya cocked her head to one side, confused.

'I want to live,' Laura continued, her tear-stained face pale, but more animated now. 'I want to feel alive, to be a part of things; have friends and do things normal people do, but I've shut myself away for so long it feels like an impossibility.' She clasped at Freya's hands. 'I'd love to help with your wedding. It's such a wonderful celebration of life, of everything that's important, but how do I face people again, when most of them are the reason I've shut myself away?'

There was something tickling at the back of Freya's mind. Something that she should know about, a memory that should never have been forgotten. And then, as she looked at Laura's beautiful face, it came to her. She squeezed her hand.

'Is your last name Ashcombe?' she asked.

There was a tiny nod as the two women leaned forward in a hug.

Five years ago, most of the farming community had turned out to attend the funeral of young David Ashcombe, a worker at the nearby Drummond Orchard, one of the largest cider producers in the area. There had been talk of dodgy working practices on the estate for years, but the general consensus was that Francis Drummond believed himself above the law and, in this case, he had seemed to get away with it. David had been killed while helping to clear damaged trees after a severe storm. The handbrake on the tractor trailer he was using had failed as he was stacking cut logs on the back. It rolled backwards crushing him to death. Laura had argued publicly that David talked frequently about badly maintained machinery, but the enquiry found it to be a simple case of operator error.

Freya's heart went out to Laura. There was nothing simple about a death, particularly of a young man with his whole life ahead of him. And the legacy that death had left behind was far from simple either, the proof was in her arms. She straightened up.

'Then we must do something to change your situation, Laura. I can't think of anything better than to have you help with our wedding, but it can't be allowed to cause you any more anguish. Let's focus on the thing you love doing most — making amazing floral arrangements and everything else we can take step-by-step and day by day. There's no need for you to have to meet anyone *en masse*. In fact, for now it'll just be me and Sam, and after that, well, whatever we do, you won't be doing it alone. How does that sound?'

Laura took a deep and calming breath. 'It sounds . . . a bit scary, but a lot less so than it did. I can't thank you enough, Freya. I'm really not quite sure what came over me.' She frowned. 'I don't normally make a habit of crying all over people and being quite so pathetic but —'

Freya put out her hand out to interrupt. 'You know, I'm a firm believer that things happen for a reason . . . often when we least expect them. A very wise man once taught me that, and when it's the right time, it really is the right time. Let's go with that, shall we, and see where it takes us. I have a feeling it might be to a very good place indeed.'

7

'And I know what you're thinking, Stephen, but back off, okay. The last thing she needs is someone beating a path to her door and declaring his undying lust for her.'

Stephen grinned. 'Are you ever going to change your opinion of me, even though you know I'm a changed man and you love me really?'

Sam looked up from yesterday's newspaper, and arched an eyebrow. 'Don't push your luck, Stephen, this is Freya you're dealing with, don't forget. She has a memory like an elephant and —'

'You say anything about the size of my backside and you're a dead man!' she exclaimed, marching between them. 'Either of you.'

Sam winked at his brother and returned his gaze to the paper. 'What did I tell you?' he muttered.

'I'm serious,' said Freya fiercely. 'Don't

even think of making any sort of advance towards Laura. She's going to need a huge amount of courage to take these first few steps, and I promised her we'd take things slowly. She certainly won't be looking for any romantic entanglements right now, especially not with someone who has all the subtlety of a brick.'

Much to Freya's surprise, Stephen nodded. 'I can't imagine what she's been through. Having David die in a horrific accident was bad enough, but then to have his integrity questioned the way it was ... it's shameful. It seems such a long time ago now, and I'm still surprised neither of us recognised her, but I do remember folks talking about it down the pub for weeks, and not in a good way either.'

Sam raised his head in astonishment, catching Freya's eye with a knowing look. 'I don't suppose they meant any harm, but folks don't always think before they open their mouths, especially if they've got a few on board at the time. I think we can all remember the time when the three of us were the subject of gossip and speculation, and it wasn't a pleasant experience. The difference was that we had other people around to protect us, to some extent. Laura's been alone with her thoughts day after day.'

'I wonder if she even knows that there were people who stood up for her at the time,' added Stephen. 'I didn't know her then of course . . . still don't,' he rubbed his chin ruefully, 'but Drummond deserves to be taken down a peg or two. He did back then, and I don't suppose anything has changed.'

'And you're going to be the man who does it, are you?' remarked Freya, knowing what Stephen was like.

Stephen shook his head. 'Uh uh. Not a chance. Think what that would do to Laura. The whole lot would be raked back up again, and she needs to move on, not be tethered to the past by that scumbag.'

Freya smiled to herself, careful not to let Stephen see. He wasn't a changed man, but he was definitely changing.

Gone was the angry, arrogant bully who Freya had despised for so many years, and in his place, was a happier and more mature man. She looked at Sam affectionately, knowing that a few short months ago the brothers could hardly bear to be in the same room as one another, let alone trade jokes and mock insults. Things were undeniably shifting; she could feel it.

As if Sam could feel her eyes on him, he looked up, shaking out the paper.

'What day were you nearly run off the road, Stephen?' he asked. 'Was it Monday?'

'Yes, why?'

Sam laid the newspaper flat on the table. 'Because you might want to take a look at this,' he said in a low voice, anxiety creasing his brow.

Sam's finger tapped on the article which was a third of the way down the page. The headline screamed out at Stephen.

Hit and run driver leaves pensioner for dead.

'Bloody hell,' he said, scanning the page for details. 'It happened about the same time, and the driver was thought to have left the village via the Witley Road . . . that's where we were.'

Freya came round the side of the table. 'What does it say?' she asked, quickly reading the article. 'Oh, but that's awful. You should have gone to the police, Stephen.'

'To say what? I really didn't see much, I was too busy a) trying to stay on my bike, b) trying not to crash into Laura, and c) . . . shouting at her,' he finished lamely. 'And apart from anything else, I didn't realise anything was wrong at the time, other than some idiot driver losing it on the bend. It wouldn't be the first time that's happened.'

'No, but you can't ignore what's in the paper; it's too much of a coincidence.'

Stephen rolled his eyes. 'I wasn't going to ignore it. Jesus, will you ever stop labelling me as a thoughtless bastard?'

He snatched up the paper, re-reading the article, while Sam gave Freya a pointed look. She dropped her eyes to the floor.

'What I was going to say,' said Stephen, 'is that although I don't remember much in the way of detail, perhaps Laura does. She was facing the road, and it's possible she saw more of the car, and sideways on too, which makes a difference. I should go and see her. Between the two of us, we might be able to come up with something.'

Freya frowned. 'This couldn't come at a worse time for her,' she said, thinking ahead. 'Suppose you are able to give the police something which would help identify who did this, imagine what a furore there'd be; reporters, families . . . courts. Laura would find it very difficult.'

'So it's okay for her not to go to the police, but different rules apply to me, is that it?' Stephen glared at her.

'I didn't say that,' she retorted.

'Maybe not, but you might as well have done. The police are appealing for witnesses; we're witnesses. What else is there to say? I know Laura will find it hard, *if* she's seen anything, which of course I don't know yet. But if there's anything that needs to be said, at least I'd be there to hold her hand.'

'Yes, I bet you would,' she snapped, as all her old feelings about Stephen came rushing back.

Sam lurched up from the table. 'Will you two stop it! For God's sake, Freya, give Stephen a break.' He took the paper from Stephen's hand. 'Besides which, my brother was speaking metaphorically, weren't you?'

He nodded sullenly.

'So let's calm down and get back to what's important here; that a serious crime has been committed, an elderly lady is very poorly in hospital, and you and Laura are potential witnesses. There's nothing else to discuss, you both need to have a long hard think about what you may or may not have seen, and then take it to the police. Let them be the judge of what's useful information.'

Freya sat down. 'I'm sorry,' she said. 'I

just don't want Laura to get hurt, that's all.'

There was a long sighing breath as Stephen joined her. 'Freya, neither do I.'

His words sat between them for a moment until Freya looked up at him. There was a softness to his eyes that she wasn't sure she had ever seen before. She nodded gently.

'I don't have a number for Laura, though, only an address. We agreed to meet tomorrow to go through the ideas she's had for the wedding, but you should probably try to see her before then.' She hesitated for a few seconds. 'I could tell you how to get there,' she added, 'or I could come with you . . .'

Sam cleared his throat. 'Actually, Freya, I could really use your help this morning. Joe Jones is bringing his crop round at nine. From what he said on the phone, there's a lot of it.'

Freya knew when she'd been outwitted. She gave a conciliatory smile. 'Okay, Stephen, you can go on your own. Laura's cottage is on the Marlowes road, just before you get to the village. There's a lane off to the right with a post box on the corner. Laura's is the last of four houses. Clarence Cottage it's called.'

'Okay, I'll find it.'

'Oh, and one more thing?'

Stephen looked up at the query in her voice.

'Before you go, change out of your running gear.'

He sucked in his stomach automatically. 'Aye aye, boss.' He grinned.

Sam waited until Stephen had closed the back door behind him before pulling Freya up from her chair.

'I'm very proud of you, you know.' He smiled, finding her lips with his.

Freya pulled away slightly. 'I don't know why,' she said. 'When I'm such a pig. I can see Stephen's trying really hard, but he still manages to rile me quicker than anyone I know,' she added.

'You'll get there,' he replied. 'It's taken Stephen a long time to square up to his shortcomings, but now that he has, we need to trust him, hard though that may be. He's learning to trust himself too, don't forget.'

'I know.' Freya sighed, looking at her watch. 'Right, come on then, we'd better make a start if Joe's coming at nine.'

Sam pulled her in closer. 'Actually,' he muttered, 'he said he might be nearer half past . . . we've got forty minutes or so to wait . . .' he said, kissing her again.

'Oh, I see.' Freya winked, kissing him back.

* * *

Laura was in the middle of making a very long list when she realised that someone was ringing her doorbell. She had a light in every room that alerted her to the fact, but engrossed as she was, they could have been standing there for quite some time before she noticed. She gave an audible tut. She was in full flow, ideas coming thick and fast and the last thing she needed was an interruption. She hastily scribbled another item on the bottom of her list in case she forgot it.

She had on her best *I can't stand here talking all day* face on as she opened the door, which deepened further when she found Stephen on her doorstep.

'What are you doing here?' she asked without thinking. It came out rather more bluntly than she had intended.

'Hello,' he signed slowly. 'How are you?'

Laura stepped back in surprise, suddenly understanding why Stephen looked so uncomfortable. He was nervous, and it was such a contrast to what she expected from him, that she didn't know how to respond.

'Fine, thanks,' she signed back.

There was immediate alarm in his eyes, and she smothered a smile.

'Is that all you know?' she asked, dropping her hands.

Stephen offered an apologetic grin. 'Pretty much,' he said. 'That and goodbye, please, thank you and sorry.'

'I can see we're going to have a scintillating conversation,' she said drily, rather enjoying watching him squirm a little.

'An interesting collection of words.'

'It was all I had time for,' he admitted. 'But I can learn more.'

A faint tingle of alarm began to sound in Laura's head. She was touched that he had even tried to learn her language, but she didn't want to encourage him. She could understand him perfectly well as it was.

'Stephen, why are you here?' she asked. 'It's very kind of you to learn a few words of sign language, but there's really no need, I can manage.'

Stephen seemed to examine her doormat for some considerable time before he spoke again.

'I wanted to see if you were okay, after what happened the other day. Apart from throwing you to the ground, I was very rude and obviously upset you. I didn't intend to.'

Laura had replayed their encounter over and over again in her head, and was rather ashamed of her own behaviour too, although she didn't want to admit it to him.

'It was the shock I expect,' she replied. 'I wasn't at my best either, so perhaps we should forget it ever happened. No harm done as it were.'

Stephen's face clouded immediately. 'Under normal circumstances, I would agree, but it might not be possible I'm afraid . . . Look, can I come in, there's something else I need to discuss with you.'

His manner had gone from relatively relaxed, albeit in a rather nervous kind of way, to pompously formal in a matter of moments, and although part of her felt intrigued, for the most part, Laura was wary. What on earth could Stephen want with her? Against her better judgement, she stepped to one side.

'We'll go in the kitchen,' she said.

Boris stood up the moment Stephen entered the room, crossing to Laura's side where he stood in front of her like a hairy protective shield. It had the desired effect; Stephen stopped dead, hovering in the doorway unwilling to go any further.

'What's the matter with you? Don't tell me you're afraid of a big dog?' she mocked, hands on her hips.

'Only ones that growl like that,' replied Stephen, trying to keep his face towards Laura, but with one eye on the dog. 'I'm just wondering if there's a bite on the end of it.'

Laura dropped to her knees in front of Boris so that she was on a level with his nose. 'Did you growl at the nasty man?' she cooed, putting her arms around the dog's neck. 'I know he pushed me over, but you can let him in okay, you don't have to eat him.'

She stood up again, waving an airy hand at Stephen. 'Go and make friends, Boris,' she said.

Stephen took several steps backwards as the dog covered the distance between them in an instant, thrusting its wet nose into the crotch of his jeans, before licking his hand.

'I suppose you enjoyed that?' Stephen remarked, trying to extricate himself.

'Of course . . . although in all serious-
ness, he was just trying to protect me,'
she added, trying to soften the blow to
Stephen's pride. 'He'll be fine now. Just
come on in and have a seat. I'll make
some coffee, shall I?'

Stephen nodded. 'No sugar, thanks.'

She turned her back, reaching for a couple of mugs, and adding coffee to both.
She was trying to decide what to say next
and by keeping her back to Stephen, she
knew she was effectively forestalling any
more conversation until she was ready to
speak. He probably deserved an apology
for her behaviour the other day; he also
deserved her thanks. She was well aware
that being thrown in the bushes was a
small price to pay for not being run over,
but she really didn't want to make a big
deal of it. It was bad enough that he was
here at all. She certainly didn't want him
to visit again.

The coffee made, she had no further
excuse to keep her back to Stephen, and
she turned round, expecting to see him
waiting patiently at the table. Instead,

he was on the other side of the room, inspecting a garland she had made a couple of days earlier and hung in her favourite spot on the wall facing the doorway. The morning sun had picked out the stems of Honesty, like slivers of silver. He held out a hand to touch one of them while she watched.

He turned to look for her, wanting to speak, and dropped his gaze in embarrassment when he realised she was staring at him. She could see his lips start to move.

'I can't tell what you're saying if your head is down,' she said gently, blushing slightly as he also coloured.

His head jerked up again. 'I'm sorry . . . I didn't think, this is harder than . . . But this is beautiful,' he said. 'I wanted to tell you. Especially this,' he added, reaching out to touch the seeds once more. 'What's it called?'

'Honesty,' answered Laura.

Stephen swallowed. 'Oh,' was all he managed.

Laura carried the mugs back to the

table and sat down, indicating for Stephen to do the same. She was about to speak when he leaned forward to touch her hand.

'You made that, didn't you,' he said. 'It's what you do.' He rubbed a hand across his mouth that was creasing into a smile. 'I should probably explain how I know that as well shouldn't I, before you think I'm some sort of psychic nutter. My future sister-in-law mentioned that she'd met you, and that you're going to help with her wedding flowers . . .' He looked at her apologetically. 'I have a bit of an unfair advantage, don't I, especially since we've never been properly introduced, but —'

'I know your name's Stephen,' interrupted Laura.

'Oh. Did Freya mention me?'

'No, I just know who you are.' She let that sit for a moment. 'And I expect that you know my name is Laura, because you've put two and two together, and after all how many deaf girls with big dogs can there be around here?'

As soon as the words had left her mouth, her eyes flickered closed in irritation. She had promised herself she wasn't going to do this. Stephen looked quite uncomfortable, and she almost missed what he said next.

'It wasn't quite like that,' he added. She could see the line of his jaw tightening.

She took in a deep breath and smiled. 'No, I know. Sorry, that came out wrong.' His teeth were still clenched.

'So, anyway, now that we don't need to introduce ourselves, I should at least say thank you for the other day,' she said as brightly as she could. 'I realised later of course that you were actually trying to do me a favour by pushing me in the bush. And if you hadn't, then either you would have hit me with your bike, or Giles would have run me over. On balance, the bush was the much better option.'

Stephen had just taken a mouthful of coffee and almost spat it across the table at Laura. He wiped his mouth as a trickle of it escaped. 'What did you say?'

he gulped.

'Well, there's no need to sound quite so surprised,' Laura retorted. 'I'm trying to apologise but if you —'

There was another touch to her hand, and she snatched it away.

'No, you misunderstood me, don't be cross, Laura. You said a name just now, what was it?'

There was a very urgent expression on his face, and Laura wondered what on earth she'd done wrong.

'What, Giles, do you mean?' she asked tentatively.

Stephen muttered something she couldn't quite make out, which probably meant he was swearing. He lowered his head to his hands, and she tutted in exasperation, flapping her hands at him.

'What did you say?' she urged. 'Why do you want to know about Giles?'

A pair of hazel-coloured eyes met hers. 'I said bloody hell,' answered Stephen. 'Because I only know of one person around here called Giles, and that's Giles Drummond. I just hope to God

I'm wrong.'

Stephen searched her expression, looking for her confirmation. He swallowed hard when he saw it.

'And you just said that Giles would have run you over . . . Are you absolutely sure the person driving the car that day was Giles? It couldn't have been anyone else?'

'Well, it's possible, but I wouldn't have thought so. What's the matter, Stephen? Why is it such a big deal, I mean everyone knows what Giles is like: too much like his father; too much money and too little sense. He has never been able to handle that car; it was ridiculous buying someone so young a machine that powerful. And half the time he's pissed out of his brain which doesn't help either . . .'

She sat back as the colour drained from Stephen's face.

'What is it, what's he done?' Her voice was like ice.

There was something like regret in Stephen's eyes. 'Do you get the evening paper?' he asked. 'Would you have yesterday's?'

Laura shook her head, unwilling to say any more.

'The reason I ask is because there was an article in it about a suspected hit and run. An elderly lady was knocked down and left for dead, and it happened about the time that I was forced off the road. No one saw the car properly, but it's thought it left the village on the Witley Road.'

Laura sat up in shock, trying to process what Stephen had just said, and then it came to her, just why Stephen was here, exactly why he had come to see her. Anger straightened her back like a ramrod.

'You must think I'm stupid as well as deaf,' she snarled. 'You didn't come here to see how I was at all, did you? With your pathetic attempt at signing and your *look at me I'm such a nice guy* act. You don't care about me one jot!' Her eyes flashed dangerously.

He baulked at this. 'That's not fair, I —'

'No,' she shouted.

'What do you mean, no?'

'No, as in, no, I won't help you. I'm not going to the police.'

'Laura, someone was seriously hurt. How can you not want to help?'

'Jesus, Stephen, are you completely thick? Who's going to listen to me? Giles Drummond is the son of the man who killed my husband. He ruined my life once, there's no way I'm going to let him do it again.'

She glared at Stephen across the table, bile rising in her throat as tortured memories of the past few years came flooding back.

'I think you'd better leave,' she said coldly.

Stephen blinked in surprise. 'What, that's it? You're not even going to consider it? How can you be so callous, Laura? She could die.'

'I might as well have, for what that man did to me.'

'But we're not talking about Francis now, we're talking about his son. Someone who has, in all probability,

105

committed a horrific crime. You can't just sit here and do nothing.'

'Watch me,' Laura spat. 'And if you're so holier than thou, you go to the police. You can still tell them what you know.'

Stephen shook his head several times. 'I don't believe you,' he said, getting up from the table. 'We all wanted to help you, but I never thought for one minute you weren't worth helping.'

'Get out of my house!' she shouted, launching herself out of her chair and pushing at his arm.

Stephen strode from the room, his long legs taking him to the door in seconds. He yanked it open and was about to slam it shut behind him when he suddenly turned and grabbed both Laura's arms.

'And you got it wrong, for what it's worth. I did come to see how you were, but I won't bother you again.' And he signed the word goodbye.

Laura stared after him, tears pouring down her cheeks before she slowly closed the door and sank to the floor.

8

Not even the sight of squirrels playing on the lawn the next morning could lift Laura's spirits. She had moved through the rest of the day before like an automaton, making chocolates, steeping more blue-black damsons in brandy, and as the golden afternoon sun had dipped behind the hedgerows, she tore up the list she was making for Freya's wedding and cried some more.

She should have known it would come to nothing, but she'd so wanted to believe that things could change. She had seen something in Freya that spoke to her, awoke a spark in her that she hadn't felt for a long time; but now all the hopes she'd had were like scalded sugar in the bottom of a saucepan, turned bitter and fit only for the bin.

Her head was full of jagged images from the past: David's coffin, impossibly small to contain a whole life, and

Francis Drummond standing over her, laughing, a gobbet of spit clinging to the end of his chin as he told her she would never win. She hadn't, and though time had done its best to ease her failure, with one fell swoop she was right back where she had started; except this time it was worse, because now she had nothing to fight for, not even David's name.

How could she possibly go to the police when all they would think — all anyone would ever think — was that she was trying to settle old scores? The thought of helping Freya with her flowers had been enough to completely unnerve her, it meant coming face to face with the people who had mocked her so cruelly; but she had allowed herself to dream, to think that things could be different and that with Freya's help, she might finally escape the past. How foolish she had been. Her bed last night had been cold and unforgiving, but she had lain in it anyway, wishing for sleep to steal her misery.

She poured a cold cup of tea down

the sink, watching the brown liquid swirl across the white porcelain of the big butler's sink. As usual, it gathered in the corners, but this morning she didn't even have the energy to wash it away. She would just have to put one foot in front of the other today and count off the hours. The graves still needed tending, and there among the undemanding dead, she might at least find some peace. She lifted her eyes to the notebook which still lay on the table, a stark blank sheet waiting to be filled. She had no idea what she was going to say to Freya later.

Stan's chocolates were in the fridge, and after Laura had collected these, together with a pot of jam for Millie and Blanche's gin, there was no further reason to hide in the house, and pulling on her jacket, she crept from the house.

She half expected Stephen to be lying in wait for her, ready with a barrage of reasons why she should change her mind, but the lane was quiet as she reached her gate. It was a beautiful autumn morning; the sky tinged pale pink and purple as the sun crested the rise of the fields beside the house. The bright orange ball hung in the still air, its golden rays filtering through the swirls of mist which clung to the grass. Within an hour the sky would be the clearest blue.

It would be a perfect day for foraging, for seeking out scarlet haws in the hedgerows, or the dusky medlars which grew in the garden of a house behind the church. A day for hurrying home to make rowan jelly and damson ketchup, but Laura knew she would do none of those things, not today.

The smile was pasted on her face as she walked up the path to Stan's cottage, but his eyesight was not what it used to be, and she doubted he would notice. She could claim a busy day, and both deliver her chocolates and collect whatever he had to offer her in a matter of minutes. No one would be any the wiser.

Her knock at the door went unanswered, and Laura automatically made her way along the path to the side of the cottage and into the back garden. It was quite usual to find Stan there, even this early in the morning, crouched beside one of his precious vegetables, or sitting in his greenhouse, letting the sun warm his bones through the glass, but she was surprised to see Millie this morning too, and Laura felt her mood sink even further. Millie's presence could only mean one thing, and Laura was in no mood for a gossip this morning, but she gave her customary wave and went to join them.

'Beautiful morning,' she called, remembering to smile.

Millie's face fell immediately. 'Oh dear,' she said, twisting a hanky around her fingers. 'You haven't heard, have you? I didn't think you had. I did call around, but perhaps you were out . . .'

'What haven't I heard, Millie?' she asked, thinking back to yesterday evening when she had studiously ignored whoever had come to her door.

Millie looked hesitantly at Stan. 'Perhaps you should tell her,' she said.

Now that she was nearer, Laura could see that both of her neighbours were not

111

their usual selves this morning. Millie looked quite upset, and Stan wore a distracted air; fidgety, not the calm, relaxed persona she was used to.

'It's Blanche,' Stan began, for some reason over emphasising the words. He had probably intended to make sure she understood them, but instead the reverse was true, and for Laura it was like listening to a transatlantic call with a lag on the line. Her brain took much longer than normal to relay the message so that she nearly missed what came next altogether. She held up a hand.

'Say again, Stan. I missed that.'

'She's in hospital,' he enunciated. 'With a broken hip and wrist.'

'She's lucky to be alive,' added Millie.

Laura stared at both of them, trying to wade through the fug in her brain. 'But I only saw her yesterday . . . No, not yesterday . . . what day is it today?'

'It's Saturday, Laura,' replied Stan, with a worried look. 'The accident happened on Monday, but none of us knew until Tuesday night when her daughter came round.'

Laura tried to piece her week back together. 'That's right, I came to see you all, on Tuesday . . . except Blanche wasn't in.' Her hand flew to her mouth. 'Oh my God.'

Stan patted her arm. 'Don't upset yourself dear, none of us knew. She'd been in hospital over a day before we found out.'

'But is she okay?'

Laura studied their faces, but neither of them said anything, just a glance flickered between the two of them.

'It's . . . difficult,' said Stan eventually, 'because of her age. The bones will heal, but the shock, well, you can imagine . . . and the doctors are worried about the risk of blood clots.'

The pit of Laura's stomach fell away. 'I've got to go and see her, where is she?'

Stan looked nervously at Millie. 'Up in Hereford, but, Laura . . . will you be all right? The police are still investigating what happened, and you know how nervous you still get around folk. There were reporters there too we heard, to start with, although maybe not now . . .'

'Police?' asked Laura, shocked. 'Why were the police involved? When you said she'd broken her hip, I assumed she'd fallen —' She stopped as she caught sight of Millie's face which was starting to crumple.

'What happened Stan? Tell me.'

'They're not sure, they think she was hit by a car.'

A slice of pain shot through Laura's head. She thrust the bag she was carrying at Stan. 'I'm sorry, I've got to go.'

Somehow, she stumbled back down the path to the front of the house, where she leaned heavily on the gate post, breathing hard. There was a wild rushing sound inside her ears, something which always happened when she was really stressed, but it was disorientating, it made her feel sick. She took several deep breaths waiting for the panic to subside. How could it be Blanche? Her lovely neighbour who had never harmed anybody. It was happening all over again — why was it always the good ones who got hurt?

If she thought she was angry yesterday, it was nothing compared with the boiling rage that hit her now, a wave of adrenaline-fuelled fury. And it was directed towards one person only: Giles Drummond. Her legs started to move of their own accord, flying first across the tarmac and then the open fields beside the church. She ran through the churchyard and out towards the Witley Road. By the time she got to Freya's house, her chest was burning, but she carried on. She hadn't reached her destination yet.

* * *

'All right, all right,' Stephen grumbled, fumbling with his trouser leg. 'Will you give me a minute, or I'll be bloody well naked.'

His wet feet refused to slide through his jeans, but eventually they made contact with the floor, and he stood up. He jogged down the stairs, doing up his fly as he went. The doorbell was still ringing.

'For pity's sake, what's so urgent,' he started, as he yanked open the door, the words dying on his lips when he caught sight of the figure standing there.

Laura was breathing heavily, eyes wild and darting, bleeding slightly from a cut on her cheek, the very last person he expected to see. A sheen of perspiration gleamed across her forehead as she stood there, her tiny figure diminished by the grand dimensions of the porch she stood under.

She held out a trembling arm. 'You've got to help me,' she said, the rest of her breath rushing from her in an anguished gasp. She looked like she was on the point of collapse.

Without thinking, Stephen pulled her through the door and into his arms. He realised too late that he would probably receive a swift and excruciating knee to the groin, but as Laura sagged against him, the seconds stretched out, and the threat of imminent pain receded. Instead, he gently rested his chin on the top of her head and wrapped his arms around her, fingers splayed but unmoving, as her tiny body shuddered against him.

He stared at the opposite wall in the hallway, focusing on the creamy expanse of paintwork and willed his body not to respond. But her fingers felt so good against his bare back, her hair against his chest . . . No! He sucked in a breath and thought about a song he had heard on the radio a few minutes ago, trying to repeat the words. Gradually, as Laura's breathing eased, and what Stephen realised were tears trailed off, he found himself relaxing. He had no idea what had brought her to his door, but whatever it was, she had asked for his help, and right now that's all he needed to give her. Whatever comfort she sought, Stephen would provide it.

It was an unusual feeling for Stephen, offering comfort to another, and not one he'd had much experience of before. Of course, he had held women in the past, snuggled up to them, but it had always been either a prelude to sex, or during

its aftermath, and he could never understand the accusations levelled at him:
*Why does it always have to lead to some-
thing else? Why can't we just have a cuddle?*
As he felt a peaceful calm envelop him
and his breathing match that of Laura's,
he suddenly got it. He understood what
he had been missing all these years, and
despite the rather unpleasant memories
of yesterday, he would stay like this forever if he could.

Whether he liked it or not, this little
spitfire of a woman had stolen a march
on his heart, and as this thought struck
him squarely, he also realised that he
would never be the kind of person who
Laura deserved in her life. With all she
had gone through, and the hurt that she
was still suffering, his loud opinions and
crass behaviour would overpower her.
So, on the day that Stephen discovered
a tiny glimmer of what it was like to fall
in love, he also realised that Laura must
never ever find out.

★ ★ ★

He'll think I'm an absolute nutter, thought Laura, and it was this which finally made her pull away from Stephen's warm embrace. When she had heard the news about Blanche, she had thought only of getting to Stephen, to tell him, to ask for his help. The anger that had engulfed her had long since gone, but in its place was a steely determination.

The Drummonds had ruined her life and stolen David's, but to leave an elderly lady for dead was more than Laura could bear. She had fought against Stephen yesterday, shock and fear replacing calm reasoning, but the last few days had taught her one thing. Just as the Drummond family had a hold on her past, the Henderson family seemed to have an equal hold on her future. She was waking up from the self-imposed sleep she'd been in for years, and although she didn't understand why things had changed, she certainly recognised that they had. There was only one person who could help her bring Blanche's assailant to justice, and that was the very man she had kicked

119

out of her house . . .

She gave a low moan of embarrassment. What on earth was she going to
say to him now?

'You're wet.' It was the first thing that
came into her head. She cringed even
more.

To her surprise, she felt Stephen's
chest rippling. He was laughing. She
looked up at his dripping wet hair.

'I've just got out of the shower.' He
grinned. 'In fact . . .' He looked down at
his bare torso. 'Maybe I should go and
get dressed. I'm practically naked.'

Laura only caught the last of his sentence as he raised his head. 'Naked?' she
asked.

'Yes, me,' said Stephen unnecessarily.
'Well not quite, but . . .'

Laura stared at the pale smooth skin
that had felt so nice under her cheek.
She blushed.

'I feel such a prat,' she groaned.
'You're going to think I'm completely
loopy; what with my performance yesterday and then coming round here this

morning, like . . . like I just did.'

'There is a somewhat marked difference in your behaviour,' replied Stephen. 'I'll give you that.' He cocked his head at her. 'So I'm guessing that something important has happened to bring about this change.' He watched her for a second or two. 'I tell you what, why don't I go and put some more clothes on, and if you like, you can make yourself a hot drink. I'll show you where the kitchen is.'

Laura nodded, glad of the opportunity for a little more time to compose herself. She followed Stephen through a door and then another, smiling politely as he showed her where the kettle and mugs were.

'And the tea and coffee are here,' he motioned, before leaving her to it.

She watched as he padded across the wooden floor, his feet bare, the bottom of his jeans slightly too long, frayed and trailing on the ground. The denim clung to his legs. Laura raised a hand to her brow. I must be in shock, she thought, that's the only explanation. But he had felt so good. She pressed the switch on the kettle. No, it wasn't Stephen that had felt so good, she corrected herself. It was simply the fact that he was a man. Tall and solid, safe even, and it been such a long time since she had been held like that. Despite the circumstances, her body had responded to a basic human need that she had been denied for so long; the simple comfort that touch can bring, that was all.

By the time Stephen returned, she was feeling more herself. Two cups of coffee stood on the work surface and she handed him one. 'No sugar, I think. Is that right?'

Stephen smiled. 'Thank you.' He'd combed his hair, and was now wearing a soft pale green shirt. 'Shall we sit down?'

He led her through to an enormous conservatory filled with plants: orchids, ferns, and a huge Stephanotis whose glorious heady scent filled the air. She looked around her in amazement.

'Are these yours?' she blurted out.

Stephen looked amused. 'Well, this is

my house, so . . .'

'I know, sorry. I just didn't think you would have plants for some reason.'

'Well, I do grow plants for a living,' he replied. 'Sort of, well, trees obviously. Although granted I do take their produce, mash it mercilessly into a pulp and make wild booze from it which I sell for inflated prices.'

Laura turned to gaze out of the window at the rows and rows of apple trees which could be seen in the distance.

'You should adopt that for your marketing literature, you know. It's quite catchy.'

Stephen crossed the room to stand in front of her. 'And you should turn back around again so you can hear me laugh,' he said.

'Sorry,' she said automatically. 'It's not really fair, is it?' She went to sit down on one of the deep squishy sofas.

'I need to apologise . . . again,' she added the minute she sat down. 'I can't begin to imagine what you must think of me and worse, I can't really explain my behaviour. Talk about hypocritical. But I'm sorry for shouting at you yesterday, for being utterly unreasonable, for coming across as a callous uncaring bitch, and for throwing you out of my house.'

'You forgot the bit where you questioned my integrity.'

Laura sighed. 'Yes, that too,' she added sheepishly, but Stephen was smiling.

'I tell you what,' he said, joining her on the other end of the sofa. 'I'm going to let you into a secret, which might not actually be all that secret, but over the years I've gained a reputation for being an arrogant womanising bastard.' He took a sip of his coffee. 'Feel free to contradict me anytime,' he said. Laura said nothing. 'See, I knew I was right. But the thing is, people usually have a reason for behaving the way they do; I know I did. It's personal to them, but other folk can't always see it for what it is; they only see the behaviour on the outside, never looking at what might have caused it.'

He checked to see she was still following him. 'The worst thing is when you decide enough is enough and try to change; people are often unwilling to give you a second chance. I don't blame them for that, but it makes it bloody difficult when you're trying to convince them of your newly reformed character. I mean I might not live that long.' He stared into his mug before looking up again. 'Look, what I'm trying to say is that I think I understand a lot of what you must have been through in the past, and how that might make you behave at times. And if you can accept that I do understand, maybe you can also accept that I can draw a line under it and start again, without the need for apology or explanation.'

Laura's heart was beating ever so slightly fast again. It seemed impossible that what Stephen was saying was true, and yet the way his eyes gazed into hers at times, she really did believe he could see into the little boxes she had stashed away in her mind. The ones that no one was allowed to open. She looked at his face now, concerned, but sincere, nothing more, and she felt her shoulders drop a couple of inches more.

'Can I ask you a question?' said Stephen, the tips of his fingers lightly tapping the mug he cradled in his lap.

She nodded, swallowing.

'When I came to see you yesterday, I was in a bit of a panic myself. I'd only just realised that we were potential witnesses to a crime and, apart from checking that you were okay, I did want to see if you could remember anything from that day. You totally floored me by saying that you actually knew who was driving the car which nearly hit us. The reasons you gave for not wanting to go to the police were valid ones, and yet today things seem . . . very different. You were obviously upset when you arrived here this morning, and if you don't want to talk about it, that's fine, but you asked for my help. Am I right in thinking that something has happened since yesterday to cause your change of heart?'

Laura smiled. 'That's very tactfully put,' she said. 'I like that you referred to me as 'upset' when you could have described me as howling and weeping like a wild banshee.'

'I thought about it.' Stephen's gaze was level.

She took a deep breath. 'I know the lady who was knocked down. I only found out today when I went to visit her, but her name is Blanche; she's a neighbour of mine and rather partial to my sloe gin. The thing is she's the sweetest, kindest lady, who wouldn't hurt a fly, and the thought of her lying there because of that evil cowardly scumbag is more than I can bear. I let the Drummond family get away with a terrible wrong in the past because I didn't have the strength to fight any more. I'm not sure I have now, but if Blanche can fight for her life, then so can I . . . only I'm not sure I can do it on my own.'

'So I'll help you.'

Laura stared at him. 'Just like that?'

'Just like that,' he replied. 'Besides which, you're forgetting that I'm a potential witness too, so I'm obliged to help, plus, I'm looking for a lost cause to support so that folks can see I've redeemed my wicked ways. I think you might do nicely.'

Laura's cheeks grew hot again. 'You're teasing me now,' she huffed. 'Stop it.'

'Only a smidge.' Stephen grinned. 'After all I need to keep you sweet — my future sister-in-law will have my guts for garters if I do anything to jeopardise her wedding preparations.'

'Oh my God!' exclaimed Laura, putting her mug down with a thump. 'Freya. I'd completely forgotten about her. I'm supposed to be meeting her this afternoon with some ideas, and I've got nothing prepared. What am I going to do?'

'I don't know. What do you need?'

'Only half the hedgerows between here and Much Marlowes.'

Stephen wedged his mug between his knees and waggled both hands. 'I'm not fit for much fancy stuff, but I can pick, will that help?'

9

Laura held her breath. 'What do you think?' she asked.

The table was covered in flowers, fruit, berries, greenery and indeed a sample from every hedge and field for miles around it seemed. At the far end, Freya sat in absolute wonder, clearly trying to take in everything she had been shown..

'It looks incredible. The colours, the smells . . . Everything is so enticing, I want it all,' she said, laughing.

'We might have gone a bit over-board,' admitted Laura, smiling at the memory of Stephen's eagerness as he gathered and picked the best of what the countryside had to offer. 'But I wanted to show you what the decoration in the marquees could look like. I have some very strong ideas for your bouquet, and these will be echoed in the more formal church arrangements, but I thought the reception could take something a little less structured. The beauty of these extended garlands is that they just grow out of whatever comes to hand at the time. There's no uniformity to them, but instead each area is worked up with a variety of colours and textures, whatever fits, pretty much.'

'What do you think, Stephen?' asked Freya.

Laura smothered a smile at the memory of Freya's raised eyebrows as she caught sight of Stephen casually leaning up against her sink earlier. A long and rather ponderous explanation for his presence followed which, in Laura's opinion, made it seem far more suspicious than it really was. In truth, she wasn't sure why he had stayed either but, as the day had worn on, her determination of the morning had begun to fade and her doubts chipped away at her again. It was only Stephen's cheerful chatter that had kept her from succumbing to her fears, and she knew that without him, she would be feeling very different.

Now, Freya's reactions to her ideas

were more than she could ever have wished for. By the time she and Stephen had returned from hunting out and collecting the various plants she wanted to use, it was the middle of the afternoon, which hadn't left her much time to think about her ideas and make up a few samples. To be honest, she had been winging it for much of their conversation, but she and Freya were so much on the same wavelength that Laura had needed only to start a sentence to have Freya finish it.

She suddenly became aware that Stephen was staring at her. He had come to join them at the table after a while, but so far had said very little.

'Sorry, did you say something?' she asked, pulling herself back to the conversation.

'Only that I've never seen anything quite like this before. And could I please have another chocolate?'

Laura pulled the tray out from beneath her notebook. She pushed it towards him.

'To be fair,' he added, 'I'm not one

to frequent florist's shops on a regular basis, so I have no idea what wedding flowers are supposed to look like.'

Freya slapped his arm. 'Don't be so rude,' she said.

Stephen looked indignant. 'I'm not being rude. You asked for my opinion, and I gave it. I have no idea what brides like these days, but in my humble opinion what we've seen here is truly beautiful. Even I can see that. The sweets are lovely too.'

'Yes, well, I'm not supposed to be eating those,' said Freya, 'or I'll never fit into my dress. But they are gorgeous. What did you say they were?'

'Blackberry and coconut cream truffles,' replied Laura.

Freya closed her eyes briefly as she let the sweet melt in her mouth. 'Well, you'll have to let me know where you get them from. When the wedding is over, I'm going to pig out on these.'

'I make them most weeks, so just let me know when you want some. It's not a problem.'

A dribble of chocolate threatened to escape Freya's mouth as she swallowed hastily.

'You make these, did you say . . . ? Oh my God, I have a friend who's going to love you.' She licked her lips. 'She runs a shop which sells gourmet handmade produce among other things. These would be perfect for her.'

Stephen leaned forward. 'Merry, of course! Why didn't I think of that? That's a seriously good idea, Freya. In fact, I'm sure Merry would be keen to stock all the other gorgeous things that Laura makes, I . . .' He sat back, catching the expression on Laura's face. 'Okay, one thing at a time . . . sorry, back to the wedding.'

Laura smiled. 'So, are you happy for me to go ahead, Freya?' she asked, steering the conversation back on track. 'If you can give me a couple of days, I can work up some proper designs for your bouquet as well, and then I'll need to get things finalised. With only two weeks to go, I'll need that time to plan how and when I'm going to get it all done.'

'I'm more than happy. You won't believe how lucky I feel to have found you,' gushed Freya. She looked as if she was about to say something more but then stopped herself. 'Are you sure you're okay with all of this? I know we're asking a lot of you.'

'I honestly don't know,' Laura admitted. 'But I do know that I couldn't have gone on like I was. You've given me an opportunity to change my life, and I've got to have faith that whatever will be, will be for a reason. And a good one, I'm sure.'

'Even so, you'll promise you'll ask for help if you need it,' said Freya. 'Or just to talk, you know, if things get tough.'

'I will, I promise.'

'And tomorrow I will metaphorically be holding your hand every step of the way,' said Stephen, with a glance at Freya. 'So try not to worry about that. The police will be sympathetic to your feelings I'm sure.'

Laura gave a weak smile. She was tired now, almost overwhelmingly so, and despite Stephen's assurances, the thought of the following day loomed large.

'Come on, Stephen, we must go,' announced Freya. 'Laura looks exhausted, and I've still got a million and one things to do today as well.' She looked at the table, still covered in piles of paper and foliage. 'We'll help you clear up first, though, if you like.'

Laura waved away their suggestion, suddenly longing for her own company. It had been quite a while since she had been with people for such a length of time, and it was exhausting just following the conversation. 'No, it's fine. I might have a bit more of a play in any case. I'll clear it away later.'

Freya came forward to give her a hug. 'Take care,' she said afterwards. 'And thank you.'

Stephen hovered awkwardly by the door. 'See you tomorrow,' he said. 'I'll pick you up at nine.' He was about to follow Freya back out into the hallway when he suddenly turned back to her.

He made a sign with his hands.

Laura's eyes widened in surprise. 'What did you say?' she asked.

'Thank you,' said Stephen, repeating the sign.

She could still see the expression on his face several minutes after she closed the door behind them.

10

'That's a pretty serious accusation to make, Mrs Ashcombe.'

Laura could feel her pulse begin to quicken once more. 'I am aware of that,' she bit back. 'I might be deaf, but there's absolutely nothing wrong with my eyes.'

The two police officers exchanged a look as Laura felt a gentle touch on her arm. She glanced at Stephen, who smiled warmly.

'From the moment I mentioned our accident to Laura, it was clear that she recognised both the car and its driver,' he said. 'And that was before she even knew about the hit and run incident. It's hardly an accusation.' He looked between the two men sitting opposite them. 'You appealed for witnesses to come forward, and we have. Until the day we were run off the road, I didn't even know Mrs Ashcombe personally, although I am of course aware of the history between her and the Drummond family. The two things are entirely unconnected, however.'

The policeman directly opposite Laura sat back in his chair, looking at her with a frown. 'And yet the last time you entered this station, it was on a charge of assault.'

Laura hung her head. She could feel Stephen's eyes on her, but really, what was the point? What was she even doing here? She felt a wave of anger balling in her chest as though it would explode from her at any minute. She drew her legs underneath her, making ready to stand. She needed to get out of here.

The pressure on her arm increased. 'When was this?' asked Stephen, as she looked up. She shrugged away his touch.

'Does it matter?' she replied. 'I told you this whole thing was pointless.' She glared back at the policeman.

'It probably doesn't matter, no,' said Stephen, 'in that it clearly has nothing to do with the reason we're here today . . . But it might help me to understand why it looks as though you're not being taken seriously. And that actually matters a very great deal.'

Laura held his gaze. She could tell from the way his lips pursed that there was a real force behind his words, and although his face was turned towards her, she understood that he was not talking to her alone. She glanced across the table, where the policeman's previously relaxed pose had been replaced with a more businesslike stance. She licked her lips and swallowed.

'I was shopping,' she said calmly, 'just before Christmas. Something I try very hard not to do, but it was a bit of a special occasion. Usually, I go home to Mum and Dad's, but last year my neighbours all persuaded me to stay here and join them for Christmas dinner. I'd had to go to the big Tesco.' She bit her lip as her face was suddenly flooded with heat. 'That's when Francis started having a go.'

'What do you mean 'having a go,'

Laura? What did he say?' encouraged Stephen.

Laura was quiet for a moment. It would sound stupid, she knew. Pathetic even. But to her, it had meant a very great deal. Staying in Much Marlowes for Christmas had been a big step for her at the time and had pretty much taken all her courage. Explaining it to complete strangers, however, would never do justice to how she had felt. She dropped her head, running a thumb over the smoothness of her fingernail. She was still staring at her hand when Stephen's fingers slipped over her own. She looked up in surprise.

'What did he say, Laura? Was he rude? Hurtful?'

She nodded gently. 'He made fun of me, it's what he always does. Goading me for being on my own; a sad and lonely creature he called me, saying it's no wonder no one wants me, looking up at people the way I do with my big doe eyes. Like I wouldn't say boo to a goose . . .

Then he made some stupid joke about geese and Christmas and that what I needed was a good stuffing . . .' The tears sprang to Laura's eyes. 'It was too much . . . especially coming from him, and it's not like it was the first time he'd done it either. I just couldn't bear it any more.'

Stephen's fingers tightened over her own. 'Bastard . . .'

The policeman nearest to her raised his hand. 'I understand that you were upset, Mrs Ashcombe. That was very clear to see when you came into the station, but it still didn't give you the right to assault the man.'

'I did not assault Francis Drummond. I threw a turkey at him, which is hardly the same thing. And you and I both know that the only reason I got dragged in here in the first place was so that you could keep your boss sweet; everyone knows he's been in Drummond's pocket for years. I bet you had a good laugh about it with him, didn't you? About how you ticked me off, and told me to behave myself. It's Drummond that needs keeping on a lead, not me.'

The two men exchanged looks. 'I rather think we're getting off the point here . . .'

'And yet it was you who brought up the subject of the assault, I believe?' interrupted Stephen. 'And as such, perhaps you could have the decency to listen to what Mrs Ashcombe has to say. At least, try looking at it from her point of view.' He turned to look Laura straight in the eye. 'I would imagine that for someone who's deaf, shopping in a supermarket just before Christmas must be hell — aside from the usual irritations, imagine what it must be like with people pushing past you, coming from nowhere because you can't hear them — glaring at you because they think you're ignoring them. Shop staff with even less time than usual tutting and sighing at their 'awkward' customer, never realising that you can't understand them. I bet their facial expressions hurt just as much as any words.' He paused for a minute to check that Laura was following him. She nodded slightly.

'Then, add to that the pain of having to spend another Christmas without the person you love, forcing yourself to be jolly and sociable which, by the way, only ever serves to reinforce the fact that you're by yourself, and you probably don't even come close to the way Laura was feeling that day. So, when a bully like Francis Drummond turns up, towering over her five-foot-three, shoving his face in hers and making rude and spiteful comments, it's no wonder she lost her temper.' He sat back in his chair, turning to look back at both policemen before returning his gaze to Laura. 'Now, given all that, she still finds the courage to come and report a crime, knowing that she probably won't be believed. And she does so not because she has a grudge against the Drummond family, but because an elderly lady has been knocked down and seriously hurt, and it's the right thing to do. I've validated everything she's described this morning about what happened on Monday, except the identity of the driver which I couldn't see. What more do you need to know?'

★ ★ ★

Laura leaned up against the wall outside the police station, gasping for breath. 'I'm sorry, I know I shouldn't be laughing, but you should have seen your face when I said I'd thrown a turkey at Drummond. It was priceless.'

Stephen caught both of her hands, pulling her upright. He faked hurt for a moment. 'I thought I'd hidden it pretty well,' he said, pretending to pout, although the corners of his mouth began to turn upwards despite his attempts at restraint. 'You have to admit, it sounded really funny the way you said it. Did you honestly throw it at him?'

'I did. It caught him square in the back of the neck,' said Laura, grinning again. 'It just came over me in a wave; I was so angry. I watched him walk away for a moment and then, boom! I picked up the nearest thing and hurled it at him — sent him sprawling. That's why he made such a fuss of course, because the place was heaving, and he went down like a sack of spuds. He did this *poor me, I'm just an innocent defenceless man struck down by a lunatic woman* routine. I couldn't tell half of what was being said of course, so I just kept shouting at him until the security guard came and hustled me away. I think they thought I was a spurned lover or something.'

Stephen was properly laughing now, his eyes shining in amusement. 'I wish I'd been there to see it —' he said, and then he stopped. 'Although if I had, things might have been a little different of course . . .' And there was that look again, the one that Laura couldn't define, but that was beginning to make her feel hot all over again.

'Anyway,' he continued, pulling away a little. 'I'm glad the bastard got what he deserved, even though it's meant you've had more of a tough time of things.'

Laura nodded back towards the police station. 'Will they do anything, do you think?'

'Oh yes, I think they got the message,' he replied, smiling. 'The local police probably don't see much more than a few kerfuffles outside the Red Lion on a Friday night. It's pretty quiet around here, and they're local lads after all, soaking up all the town gossip just like anyone else. Their attitude was somewhat different by the end of our conversation, don't you think?'

'Thanks to you,' Laura remarked. 'That was some speech.'

Stephen thrust his hands into his pockets and swallowed hard. 'I wanted them to treat you properly, that's all.' He dropped his head and mumbled something Laura couldn't catch.

'What was that?' she asked, deliberately forcing Stephen to look up again.

'I said, it's only what anyone would do,' he repeated.

Laura held his look for a second before replying. 'Really?' she queried.

'Only no one has done anything like that in the last five years.' She looked up and down the street again, conscious of Stephen's eyes on her face. 'I tell you what,' she said, breaking the awkward silence. 'Why don't I buy you a coffee as a thank you? And the biggest piece of cake we can find. It's the least I can do after you stuck up for me like that.' She was pleased to see Stephen looked relieved.

'Deal,' he said, with a quick glance to his watch, 'and then I've got to go and see a man about a disco of all things, I'm afraid. I'm Sam and Freya's official wedding entertainment co-ordinator, God help them.'

Laura smiled. 'Yes, I must get back too. Wedding bouquets to design and all that.' She cleared her throat. 'Is Mrs Muffin's Tearoom okay? It's the only place I've ever been in.'

Stephen offered her his arm. 'That will do fine,' he said. 'I'll avoid the rock cakes, though. That way if the conversation takes a turn for the worse, I won't end up with concussion.'

11

Stephen drummed his fingers against the steering wheel. He'd been stuck behind the tractor for what seemed like an age now, and whilst he hadn't made any firm arrangement over what time he'd call in to confirm the disco booking, he was later than he'd planned, and getting later by the minute.

It was partly his fault of course. His joke to Laura about the rock cakes had set her laughing again, and it had been so good to see her serious face lift and relax. If he was honest, he was also rather relieved at having managed to turn the conversation back to something more light-hearted, rather than focusing on his behaviour at the police station. That conversation had danger written all over it, and he had been anxious to move away from all that it might have implied. Laura didn't need those kind of complications in her life right now, and Stephen had been so surprised by how he had felt sitting next to her in the station that he had shoved these thoughts firmly to the back of his mind.

Of course, this lightening of the mood, welcome though it was, had also meant that a quick coffee had turned into the best part of an hour-and-a-half as the conversation flowed. Now, he couldn't remember half of what they had talked about, and that was something he didn't want to think about either. He wasn't used to feeling like this, hadn't in fact at any time in his life so far, and the thought was more than a little unnerving. He didn't know what to do with himself. He focused on his driving, and switched on the radio. He knew the road ahead like the back of his hand and there was no way he was going to get past this trac-tor. He was here for the duration, and he might as well try to find something to distract himself with.

He fiddled with the radio until he found a station playing eighties songs. As a small child, their kitchen had always been the place for music, his mother's tinny radio blaring it out from its permanent place on the windowsill. He'd never really bothered much with music over the years, and they were still the songs he knew best. As he'd grown older, he'd swapped the kitchen for the pub, or gone to clubs and parties. Records had been the background to much of life, and yet he was ashamed to think how little he'd appreciated what he heard. In a few minutes, he'd be finalising the music for his brother's wedding reception, and he had no idea what he wanted, what Sam and Freya would want. It was a stark reminder that so much in his life to date had been given so little thought. The only things he had cared about were his own selfish desires.

He caught sight of himself in the wing mirror as he peered around the tractor and looked away. He had taken so much for granted: wealth, his home, his family. Even women, attracted at first by what they saw on the outside. They never stayed long of course, once they got to know Stephen, but that had never mattered. Plenty of sex and no commitments had suited him just fine. But now he wondered what it must be like to have none of those things? To love someone so much that the pain of being without them was almost unbearable, to have to fight for every penny, to feel alone almost every day, because an invisible disability distanced you from the world. Even the joy of music or birdsong was denied you. He pulled up behind the tractor as it stopped at the end of the road and switched the radio off. He had time to make a difference, he thought, as he turned the opposite way to the tractor and accelerated out onto the clear road. Not much time admittedly, but it would have to be enough.

* * *

'It's a good job, I've known Sam since we were five,' joked Ash, 'you're bloody hopeless.'

Stephen pulled a face. 'Tell me

something I don't know,' he said, frowning. 'Actually, tell me it's not a problem and that you know exactly what music to play despite my lack of input.'

Ash chewed the end of the pen he was holding. 'Maybe now might be the time to tell you that I bumped into Sam at the petrol station last week, and he gave me a bit of a heads-up. He mentioned you might be clueless.' He smiled. 'In the nicest possible way of course . . . so we'll be fine. I'll get them all up and dancing, don't worry, and I've come up with the perfect song for their first dance so even that's sorted.'

Stephen looked up sharply. 'Oh God, is that a thing?' he groaned. 'How was I supposed to know that?'

Ash grinned. 'I think you might need to brush up on your best man's duties . . . although I don't suppose you ever thought you'd be needing to, what with . . . well, everything that went on—' He stopped for a moment, his face falling. 'Sorry, mate, I didn't mean . . .'

Stephen shrugged. 'It's okay,' he said.

'It was a long time ago. A lot of water under the bridge, and me and Sam are good now. Freya too, actually.' He swallowed.

'Yeah, he mentioned that,' replied Ash, with an answering nod. 'I'm glad that things worked out . . .'

'Me too. Freya and I . . . well, it would never have worked. I know I've been a dick most of my life, but I'm genuinely glad she's with Sam; it's where she was always meant to be. It's just unfortunate that despite my best intentions now, Sam still has a shit best man.' He pulled his wallet from his jacket pocket. 'At least I can do one thing, though, and that is pay you. What did we say, two hundred and fifty quid, wasn't it?' He pulled out a roll of bank notes and placed them on the desk in front of him. 'And you know where you're going, don't you? The marquee will be up from the Thursday before, so you can set up whenever suits you.'

Ash pulled out a money tin from a drawer beside him. 'Yeah, I'll shout if I have any problems. Hang on a sec, and I'll print you out a receipt.' He turned his computer screen back towards him and clicked the mouse that lay on the desk beside it. A printer behind him whirred into life, and he passed the single sheet of paper it produced across to Stephen. 'Cheers, mate. Another one to add to your pile, no doubt.'

Stephen glanced at the paper before folding it in half. 'Thanks, Ash,' he said with a grimace. 'Now I'll just go and worry about all the other things I'm supposed to be doing.' He rose from his chair and crossed the tiny office from which Ash ran his business. The door was half-open before he noticed the poster that was stuck on the back. He stopped for a moment, before turning back towards the room. 'This is something new, is it?' he asked, tapping the poster.

'Oh, aye,' nodded Ash. 'Got to move with the times, my friend. Actually, they've been really popular. Good for a giggle and all that, especially when folks have got a few on board if you know what

I mean.'

Stephen looked down at the receipt in his hand. 'Yeah, I bet,' he said, thinking out loud. 'I don't really know much about them,' he added. 'How do they work exactly?'

★ ★ ★

It was probably the worst idea he'd ever had. It was rash at the very least, but now that he'd done it, he couldn't get the idea out of his head. The thought of Laura's face when she realised what was happening, what it might lead to ... Stephen groaned out loud and shifted uncomfortably in his seat. He rested his head on the steering wheel and took deep breaths. Dear God, what on earth was the matter with him? He couldn't sit in their driveway for long; any minute now Freya would look out of the kitchen window and spot him. But how on earth was he going to go inside and tell her, and Sam for that matter, that he'd just completely hijacked their plans for their wedding reception? And that wasn't all he'd done either.

He lifted his head and glanced down at his groin, checking that he had everything under control. Knowing how protective his future sister-in-law was of Laura, there was no way he could enter their kitchen in his current state. He was in for an earbashing as it was. He refocused his mind very firmly, and reluctantly climbed from the car.

As it turned out, the kitchen was empty when he pushed open the door, and a bout of loud yelling through the house brought no response either. Freya and Sam must both still be outside, which was a pity; he'd rather hoped that he'd be able to get either one of them on their own. He doubled back on himself, past the car and across the yard to the big barn that lay along one side of it. This too was empty, but as he neared the large open doors on the far side, voices floated through from outside. He groaned again. This was really not going well.

She had her back to him as he emerged outside, but he could hear her soft voice trail off as she caught sight of Freya's expression which changed to one of greeting as soon as she saw him. Laura turned around, and he saw her cheeks coloured pink by whatever excitement had lifted her voice too. She was holding a bouquet in her hands.

'I'd forgotten you were coming!' exclaimed Freya, giving him a beaming smile. 'Because look what Laura's brought over to show me. Now I'm that bloody excited I can't stand still.' And as if to illustrate her point, she gave a little hop. 'What do you think? Isn't it the most beautiful thing you've ever seen?'

Stephen, who was looking at Laura, could only nod. It wasn't until Freya took the bouquet from Laura's hands offering it to him that he realised he was supposed to say something. He took the bouquet, feeling the coolness of the blooms against his skin, the rosy apples mingled with creamy flowers, scarlet hips and dusky blackberries. There wasn't anything he *could* think of to say.

'It's just a rough one,' said Laura. 'You know, to give you the idea of how it might look, what we might use.'

Stephen nodded again. 'It doesn't look rough,' he managed. 'It looks perfect . . . I couldn't quite grasp what you meant when you described it to me this morning, but now . . .' He was aware of Freya staring at him from the corner of his eye, but he couldn't look at her.

'I'd forgotten that you two had already seen one another today,' said Freya, taking hold of Laura's arm. 'How did that go? Come on, we can go and put the kettle on, and you can tell me all about it.' She beamed at Stephen. 'And bring that, I don't think I can bear to let it out of my sight.'

Fortunately for Stephen, Laura and Freya were so excited that he hardly needed to say a word, which was just as well considering that his ability to speak had somehow deserted him. Unfortunately, however, Laura's excitement at Freya's reaction to her flowers spilled over into her recounting their time in the police station that morning, and so instead Stephen had to sit squirming at every mention of his name.

'Well, I hope they string the bastard up,' declared Freya. 'And well done you, Stephen, for sticking up for Laura. I had no idea that all this with Francis had gone on before, but then I don't suppose many people do. I hate the way he does business and most of the growers around here would probably say the same, but that's entirely different. I had no idea what a horrible man he was personally.' She took a sip of tea from the mug in front of her. 'As far as Giles is concerned, I've always thought there's truth in that old saying that *the apple doesn't fall very far from the tree*.' She took Laura's hand. 'Have you heard how your friend is doing?'

Laura shook her head. 'No, I was planning on going to see her tomorrow,' she replied, running a finger around the bottom of her mug. 'I've been putting it off, to be honest . . . I don't have very fond memories of that hospital.' She gave an apologetic smile. 'But I must go, Blanche was very good to me when David died.'

'Well, Stephen can go with you, can't you, Stephen? That would help, surely, having some company.'

Stephen couldn't believe it. He tried to glare at Freya without Laura noticing, but of course she had her eyes fixed on his face, so it was impossible. It wasn't that he didn't want to go, far from it in fact, but simply that the way he was feeling right now, being around Laura for too long probably wasn't a great idea. If only Freya hadn't blurted it out the way she had. Perhaps if she'd run it by him first, he could have tactfully made an excuse, or at least let her understand some of his . . . difficulties . . . but there was nothing for it now. He fixed a bright smile to his face.

'Well, that sounds sensible. I'm more than happy to go with you, Laura, if that's okay with you of course.'

And just as he knew she would, she smiled and accepted his offer.

'Would one o'clock be okay?' she asked. 'Only visiting starts at two.' She gulped down the last of her tea. 'Right, well, I must be off while there's still enough light to pick some more sloes. Thanks ever so much, Stephen. I'll see you tomorrow.' She leaned over to give Freya a hug. 'And we must meet up again soon too. I'll need some more apples for one thing.'

The door hadn't quite closed before Freya placed both elbows on the table and leaned forward, her hands making a cradle under her chin.

'You know it pains me to say it, Stephen, but I think Laura rather likes you. I've still got my eye on you, mind, but what you did today was really generous, and it's definitely earned you some brownie points. Now, what did you come over for again? With all the excitement of the wedding plans, I've completely forgotten.'

Stephen eyed her wearily from across the table. 'Nothing really,' he said. 'Just a bit of a catch-up, that's all.'

12

Laura dragged a tissue across her lips, grimacing at herself in the mirror. Since when had she ever worn lipstick? Once upon a time, she told herself, a very long time ago, and she had no intention of starting again today. It wasn't as if Blanche would even notice, so she could stop fooling herself that her neighbour was the cause of her madness. The trouble was, she wasn't fooling herself; she knew exactly what the reason was, and his name was Stephen.

She stared at her reflection angrily. *Yes Stephen, no Stephen, three bags full Stephen,* she mimicked. For heaven's sake. Anyone would think she was a hormone-laden teenager the way she was carrying on, and most importantly what would Stephen think? He must be horrified by her behaviour. The first sign of a man who doesn't want to run a mile from her, and she throws herself at his feet. And what's worse is he's just being friendly, she reminded herself; no doubt because she was providing the flowers for his future sister-in-law's wedding, and wasn't that what the best man was supposed to do? Keep the *staff* sweet, chat up the single bridesmaids, and so on. It was a role that almost had its own job description, and she had fallen for his charming charade. Pathetic.

She tugged at her fringe and thrust her hairbrush back into its pot. She just had time for some toast before she'd need to leave for the hospital. And she'd make sure there was no necessity to stop for coffee and cake today either. Having Stephen accompany her to the hospital would certainly make things easier for her, there was no doubt about that, but that's where it ended. They were going to visit her dear friend, and that's what she should focus on. She peered at herself again, narrowing her eyes in appraisal. It's just that yesterday had been such a good day in many ways, and she really couldn't remember the last time anyone had made her laugh like that . . .

Boris alerted her to the ring of the doorbell, bang on the hour, and although she had been pacing the floor for a good ten minutes, she made sure that it took her at least another minute to answer the door. She was so determined to be welcoming but not gushing, friendly but not overly so, that the expression on Stephen's face when they finally came face to face threw her completely.

'Oh,' was all she could manage. 'Is everything all right?'

He gave her a searching look. 'Can I come in?' he asked unnecessarily, hovering slightly on the threshold.

Laura opened the door wider, allowing him to pass, and stared at his broad back as she followed him down the hallway. They came to rest in the kitchen, Stephen standing rather awkwardly with one hand on Boris's head, who despite the tension in the air was trying to surreptitiously chew his fingers. Stephen didn't seem to notice. He waited until Laura was standing facing him before he spoke. He must have cleared his throat because she saw his Adam's apple rise and fall a couple of times before his lips started to move.

'I wanted to apologise for yesterday,' he started, 'because I think it may have given you the wrong idea . . .'

Laura's heart sank. Even though she had been thinking much the same thing all morning, she would have preferred to be the one to say it. The thought distracted her for a moment.

'Sorry, say again, I missed the first bit.'

Stephen smiled softly. 'No, I'm sorry,' he said. 'I was talking about the police. I think I rather took it for granted that Giles was guilty, and perhaps you did too? Of course, all the police said they would do is look into the matter, and it never occurred to me to think anything else. I'm afraid it was my fault you ended up with the impression that it would all be okay — it was me, trying to be the big I am as usual.'

Laura stared at him. What on earth was he talking about? She frowned then as the meaning of his words sunk in. 'I'm not sure I'm following you,' she said. 'Isn't everything okay? And anyway, what do you mean *taking it for granted that Giles was guilty*? He is guilty; I saw him!'

'Laura . . . Giles has a watertight alibi for Monday, the police questioned him yesterday. They rang me this morning to tell me.'

She opened her mouth and then closed it again. 'But that's not right,' she blurted out. 'How can it be?'

Stephen's expression was full of contrition, and something else too. Something she really didn't like the look of.

'I don't know, Laura, I know how positive you are that Giles was driving the car that day, but . . . I'm not quite sure where that leaves us now.'

Her cheeks began to burn. 'Don't you dare!' she fired at him. 'Don't you dare say you believe me when you clearly don't. And if you ever look at me like that again, I swear I'll throw you out. I don't need your pity.'

'Laura, I —'

She turned her back on him. 'Leave me alone,' she said, trying to stop the rush of tears that were threatening to spill down her face. She stared at the wall, her fists clenched, fighting to stay in control.

She wasn't sure which emotion she felt the most. There was anger certainly, both at the police for giving her news she didn't want to hear, and at Stephen for swallowing what they'd said without challenge, and for pitying her because she'd got it wrong again. But there was also sorrow, because she'd let Blanche down, and because she *had* got it wrong again, clearly. Just when she felt things had begun to look a little brighter, she was right back where she'd been before; the pathetic deaf girl making a huge fuss over nothing again.

She shook her head, trying to clear her confusion. This wasn't right. None of this felt right; she'd been so sure. The minutes stretched out without interruption as she stared ahead, feeling her emotions swirling round her. She tried to pick one to focus on, but they were as elusive as butterflies.

A few more seconds ticked by, moments which became increasingly uncomfortable. She'd led them both into an impasse she realised.

Either she would have to turn around, or Stephen would have to do something to attract her attention. Both these options would feel stilted and unnatural and, worse, require some kind of capitulation, and she wasn't ready to give in, not yet. Any minute now there'd be a tug to her arm, just as there had been on the day of the accident. She waited but none came, and she could feel her anger beginning to rise again.

She whirled around, an accusation ready on her lips, and was astonished to find the kitchen empty; both Stephen and her dog had gone. Her anger subsided in seconds as a healthy dose of remorse replaced it. She hadn't meant for Stephen to leave, not really, and anxiety quickened her heartbeat as she realised that she couldn't bear for him to have left.

They must have gone out into the garden. From there, the side gate led out to the path beside the house and back down the driveway. Stephen could so easily be halfway down the lane by now. She flung open the back door and rushed outside. Seated on her small bench under the kitchen window was Stephen, his long legs stretched out in front of him, his eyes closed against the warm autumn sun which slanted across the lawn. One hand rested on Boris's head which lay gently in his lap. His eyes flew open as he heard her stumble out, his legs scrambling to tuck themselves beneath him so that he could sit up straighter.

'I thought you'd gone,' she said, her eyes wide with panic.

'No,' said Stephen with a soft smile. 'I'm still here. You said you wanted to be left alone, that was all.'

'Did I?' she replied, 'I don't remember.'

Another smile. 'You did. You were quite clear.'

Laura pressed her lips together. 'Oh . . . I was worried that you'd gone, as in completely gone.'

'Well, I thought about it . . . but I hazarded a guess you didn't mean for me to leave you alone forever and, as you didn't actually throw me out, I thought I'd stay. There is still time to throw me out of course.'

She nodded slightly, not knowing what to say. She should apologise she knew that, but she couldn't quite find the right words.

Stephen shuffled imperceptibly sideways on the bench. 'Perhaps you should come and sit down while you think about it,' he said. 'It's quite nice and warm here in the sun.'

Boris lifted his head as if to make room for her too. There really was nothing else she could do, so she edged onto the seat, keeping her knees pressed together.

'You should close your eyes for a bit; stretch out,' said Stephen, releasing his legs out from under the bench again. He laid his head back against the wall. 'It's such a beautiful day.'

Laura did as she was told. The gentle heat was soothing, and she could feel her tension begin to slide away. After a few minutes, she felt Stephen's fingers brush against her own. She opened her eyes to find him looking at her.

'Would you possibly do something for me?' he asked. 'In return for my being such an obedient soul.'

She nodded. 'I might.'

'Sit here quietly — quietly mind — without interrupting, while I try to explain what I attempted to a few minutes ago. Only this time I'm going to do it as I originally intended; without upsetting you, or giving you the impression that I don't believe you, or, God forbid, that I pity you.'

Laura's stomach gave a lurch, but she nodded again, her mouth firmly closed.

'I feel really awful about yesterday,' began Stephen. 'I was furious with the way you were treated by those two policemen, and I think I lost sight of the reason we were there, ironically the same thing I accused them of. I was so determined to prove a point to them ... and if I'm honest ... well, I wanted to score a few brownie points with you too. That's my innate macho arrogance getting the better of me I'm afraid.' He rubbed a finger along a furrow in his brow. 'When we came back outside, it felt like we'd scored a victory, and I never gave much thought to the consequences of our visit — because to me you were never anything other than one hundred per cent certain of Giles' guilt, and therefore so was I. It never even occurred to me that the police would find differently, and, if they did, how difficult this would be for you. And now I don't know what to say, because they *don't* believe Giles is guilty, and you *do* feel awful, and that's probably all my fault.'

Laura looked down at her hands in her lap, and those of Stephen lying inches away from her own. Slowly, she moved one hand to cover his.

'I'm sorry too,' she said. 'Just not half as eloquently as you. But, I am very grateful you're still here, and that I haven't managed to frighten you off completely, despite my best efforts. I'm just not sure how to say the rest of it.'

'Well, how about if I say that I think I already understand, and we'll work the rest out as we go along. How does that sound?'

Laura grinned. 'Much better than anything that will come out of my mouth . . .'

Stephen returned the smile. 'Right, well, are we going to sit here all day or are we going to see Blanche?'

Laura stared incredulously at Stephen for the second time that day. 'You're actually still going to come with me?' she asked, 'After the way I've behaved?'

'I know, sometimes I surprise myself. I thought I would have shouted a few profanities by now and gone down the pub. Instead, I find myself still here which is pretty impressive given my poor track record in being a kind and compassionate human being. Funny old world, isn't it?'

The heat was rising to her cheeks

again, but this time not in anger. She looked at Stephen's easy smile. 'I'll get my coat, shall I?'

★ ★ ★

The journey to the hospital was silent for both of them, which was fine by Stephen. It gave him time to analyse the whole new barrage of thoughts that were swirling around his brain. Laura wasn't so much complicated as like a tangled ball of string. He wondered idly if he would ever be able to unpick all the knots, or indeed why he would want to, which was the strangest thing.

He had felt genuinely shocked at the news the police had given him. He honestly had not given a thought to Giles's supposed guilt or not. He had believed that it was simply a matter of letting time take its course before the inevitable arrest came; but now he felt more confused than ever. He didn't doubt Laura's certainty for a second, but he could see clearly how now, more than ever, that her previous dealings with the Drummond family stood every chance of being dragged up again, and that thought worried him a great deal. There was still the matter of a serious unsolved crime of course, and as furtive glances at Laura in the car had confirmed, she was still distraught at what had happened to her friend.

It wasn't only concern for Blanche of course. For Laura, the trip to the hospital was taking her right back to a time she had fought hard to forget. It was bound up in tortured memories of her husband teetering on the edge of life, unable to respond to her, leaving Laura unsure whether her final words to him had even been heard. He had learned the story from Freya; how David had clung to life for two long days, the medical staff doing everything they could to heal his broken body, even though his death had been all but guaranteed from the moment he had been brought into hospital. Without her hearing to help her, Laura had missed so much of what had been going on, and had had to fight for every scrap of information she could get. It must have been a hellish void. He risked another glance at her, determined that if she needed support, he would provide it. Just so long as she actually wanted it of course . . .

The walk up to the orthopaedic ward seemed to take forever, and Stephen willed every turn of the corridor to lead them to their destination. Laura was palpably tense, and more than anything he longed to take her hand, but her closed body language shouted *don't touch me* louder than words ever could. He too was beginning to get a little nervous about what they might find when they entered the ward.

In the end, he need not have worried. They eventually found Blanche at the end of a small bay, tucked into the corner under a huge window and beaming at a vivacious blonde who sat beside her bed. He hovered for a moment, unsure what to do for Laura's sake, until Blanche's visitor caught sight of them and got up immediately, a welcome smile on her face.

'Mum, you are popular today!' She laughed. 'Look, someone else has come to see you.' She held out her hand. 'I'm Elizabeth, Blanche's daughter,' she added by way of explanation.

Stephen stood back to let Laura shake the proffered hand. 'Hi,' she began shyly, 'I'm Laura, one of Blanche's neighbours . . .'

The smile widened in recognition. 'Yes, I think we've met once or twice, haven't we? And of course, I've heard all about you, or rather I've heard all about the magical properties of your sloe gin.'

Laura gave Stephen a hesitant look. 'I thought about bringing a bottle along with me today . . . but I didn't think it would be allowed . . .'

'You're probably right. Pity though, eh, Mum? You'd have liked a drop of that.'

Stephen glanced at Blanche who was lying flat on her back but, apart from a bright pink bandage circling her wrist, looked surprisingly none the worse for wear.

She waved at Laura with her good arm. 'Come and sit down, dear,' she said, patting the chair beside the bed where her daughter had been sitting. 'That's all right, Elizabeth, isn't it? That way I can talk to Laura properly.'

Elizabeth flashed Stephen a knowing smile. 'Perhaps you and I could go and find some other chairs?' she suggested smoothly. 'That way Laura can have Mum to herself for a few minutes without us all gabbling at once.'

Stephen felt his shoulders relax. 'If you're sure, you don't mind. We've rather barged in on your visiting time.'

'Oh, I've been here most of the day, don't worry. We're just waiting for the doctor's round so that mum can be discharged. She's coming home to me for a bit, until she's properly on her feet. Come on and I'll fill you in.'

She led the way back down the ward, her heels clicking on the floor. Despite the fact that Elizabeth wasn't too far off being old enough to be his own mother, she was a very attractive woman, and

178

at any other time Stephen would have admired the sway of her hips in her tight jeans, or the cashmere jumper which clung to all the right places, but not today. He was only concerned with how Laura was feeling.

'That was very kind, thank you,' he said, as they reached the corridor outside.

Elizabeth turned. 'Not at all,' she replied. 'Mum told me that Laura's deaf, but aside from that I've got a bit of an ulterior motive I'm afraid. That's why I wanted to talk to you by yourself.'

Stephen looked back down the row of beds.

'Oh?' he said.

'Since her accident, I've been in to see Mum most days, and she's really quite worried about Laura. To be honest, I'm rather ashamed that I hadn't realised what good friends they are, or that Laura had been calling in on Mum nearly every day to check on her. Physically, mum's going to be fine. She's as tough as old boots actually, but the doctors are more concerned about her up here at the moment.' She tapped the side of her head. 'At her age the shock of the accident and a bad fall can be a real setback, and couple that with the fact that she's not going to be going at the same speed as she used to, the effect on her mental health could be disastrous. A young lad came to visit Mum earlier today and since then she's been quite distressed about Laura's well-being. That's why I'm so glad to see her; it might help to put Mum's mind at rest . . . particularly now that you've come with her. Mum mentioned that Laura was on her own, you see.' She gave Stephen an apologetic smile. 'Are you — ?'

'No,' replied Stephen quickly. 'I'm Stephen — just a friend. I live in the same village and we . . . it's a long story.'

Elizabeth gave him rather too long a look for his comfort. 'Well, whatever, Mum will be glad to see you. Perhaps now she can see that Laura has someone to call on if she needs to, it will help assuage her worries. She seemed quite concerned about her living by herself, and being so vulnerable.'

They had come to rest by a stand of chairs, and Stephen automatically plucked two from the top of the pile. 'What do you mean?' he asked. 'Laura lives quite independently.'

'Yes, exactly,' Elizabeth replied. 'Mum wasn't worried that Laura couldn't cope or anything like that, more that it had something to do with this chap. I don't think she particularly liked him, although he seemed perfectly pleasant, but she mentioned something about an old family feud. Was he some dodgy boyfriend or something?'

Stephen looked at her concerned face. 'Laura doesn't have a boyfriend, she's a widow.'

Elizabeth touched her mouth automatically. 'Oh, I'm sorry,' she replied. 'I didn't know. Well, it can't have been that then.'

'No, I guess not,' replied Stephen. 'But, as you say, a good chinwag will do them both good.' He adjusted the grip on the chairs and motioned with his head.

'After you,' he said, his mouth set in a thin hard line as he followed Elizabeth back down the ward.

He did his best, but there was no way he could keep changing the subject; he was running out of things to say. So he sat, anxiously waiting for the moment when either Blanche brought up the subject of her earlier visitor, or Laura asked about the accident. Discussion of either one was guaranteed to reveal the identity of the 'mystery' young man who had come to see Blanche, at which point it would propel Laura through the ceiling. All Stephen could do was hang on until it did, and do his best to deal with the fallout. That, and pray for a miracle.

'He must think I'm soft in the head, or something,' Blanche deduced after a few minutes of animated discussion. 'As if that lad would even think about somebody else, let alone come and visit an old biddy in hospital, and one he hardly knows at that.' She looked across at Elizabeth. 'And I'm not surprised one little bit. His father's just as bad, as you very well know, Laura.'

Elizabeth looked confused. 'I'm sorry, Mum, I'm not following you. Are you saying that this lad who came in earlier is the one who knocked you down? Because that's a very serious accusation. I thought you didn't see the car?'

Blanche tutted. 'I didn't, but why else would he come to see me? He wanted to see if I remembered him of course; no doubt worried he's going to get into a whole heap of trouble. I think I did pretty well not letting on.' She smiled gleefully.

All of three of them exchanged looks; Laura now sitting up ramrod straight and Elizabeth opening and closing her mouth.

'But Mum, you have no proof. You can't make wild accusations like that, he could have come for any number of reasons ...'

It was inevitable really, Stephen knew that. And the fact that he'd seen it coming a mile off didn't help. The conversation had been brewing like a volcano waiting to explode, and there was nothing

Stephen could do to stop it. He looked at Laura, stricken, knowing exactly what was going to come out of her mouth any minute now.

'Did he actually say anything out of the ordinary to you, Blanche?'

The old lady shook her head. 'No . . . but then he wouldn't, would he, not with Elizabeth here. Of course, he didn't stay long, there was no point really. He couldn't get what he came for.'

To his astonishment, Laura chuckled. 'Would you listen to yourself, Blanche! I think you've been reading too many Agatha Christies.' She glanced at Elizabeth. 'I'm sure the police are doing everything they can to find out who did this, but for now the most important thing is for you to forget all about the accident and concentrate on getting better. Have some lovely time with your daughter and get fit and well again. After all, I shall still need a good home for my sloe gin, and who else is going to drink it?'

Elizabeth reached over and squeezed

her mum's hand. 'She's right, Mum. I'm going to enjoy spoiling you rotten, so you're not to worry about a thing.'

'And I shall be making sure that Laura's well looked after whilst you're not around to keep an eye on her,' said Stephen. 'So, no fretting about that either.'

Laura checked her watch. 'We should get going really. You've had a busy day already, and we don't want you to be too tired to enjoy getting out of this place.' She got up and planted a kiss on Blanche's cheek. 'You behave yourself now and do what Elizabeth tells you. I'll see you very soon.'

A few moments later, after general goodbyes and promises to keep in touch, Stephen found himself hurtling down the corridor after Laura, trying to keep up with her. Much as he hated doing so, the only way he could get her to slow down was to catch her hand. She swung to face him.

For a moment, he thought she might be about to belt him one, such was the look of fury on her face, but then to his amazement her face broke into a wide smile.

'Sorry,' she said, almost breathless. 'You're right, I should stop, calm down . . . otherwise . . .'

'You'll nail the bastard to a tree?' suggested Stephen.

Her shoulders dropped. 'Something like that,' she said with a wry smile. 'You're also sure that it was Giles who came to visit today?'

'I'm afraid so, yes,' replied Stephen. 'I think it was pretty obvious.' He looked at her flushed face for a moment. 'You know that was a stellar piece of acting back there — letting Blanche think she was imagining things. It was a kind thing to do.'

'Well, I could hardly agree with her, could I? Imagine how she would feel.' She tilted her head to one side. 'You know something, Stephen Henderson . . .' She paused for a second as if thinking of what to say. 'Nah, don't worry, it doesn't matter.' And with that she took hold of his hand again, and started to walk. 'Come on. We've got things to do, and first on the list is to call the police. I think they might be very interested to learn of Giles' antics this afternoon.'

13

Freya wiped a dribble of melted butter off the end of her chin. 'Just think ...' She sighed happily. 'In four days' time I will be making your bacon sandwiches as Mrs Henderson. What do you think of that?'

Sam took another huge bite of his breakfast, chewing slowly and thoughtfully. 'Will you be changing the recipe at all?' he asked eventually. 'Only if you do, I fear it may be grounds for divorce.'

'And why would I mess with perfection?'

'Why indeed ...'

They sat in silence save for the occasional slurp of tea, and the ticking of the huge grandfather clock which stood in one corner of the kitchen. Freya, who already had one eye on it, sighed again. How was it already seven o'clock in the morning? She'd been up since four and the To-Do List, which sat ominously in the middle of the table, still had just as many items to get through as it had when she first woke up. 'I could go back to bed; I don't know about you.'

Sam put the last of his sandwich down on his plate. 'Jeez Freya, again? I'm not sure I can keep up with your demands.' He winked cheekily, and Freya stuck out her tongue.

'Oh, ha, ha,' she replied, ignoring his expression. 'Not a chance, mate. We've still got far too much to do . . . In fact, I'm thinking of imposing a ban on sex until after the wedding — seeing as it was you who suggested it would be a good idea to get married in the middle of the harvest . . .'

'Freya Sherbourne, you bloody liar! It was all your doing, as well you know, romantic fool that you are.'

'Me?' she queried, with mock innocence. 'It can't have been me. I would never have suggested anything so daft.' She met his look with eyes that danced with good humour. 'Come on, eat up, we haven't got all day.'

'Mutter mutter, grumble grumble; bloody slave driver,' said Sam with a smile, getting up from the table. He offered a solicitous hand to his soon-to-be wife. 'Listen, about the whole sex thing, maybe we could renegotiate . . .'

Freya was pulling on her wellies when a thought occurred to her. 'Have you heard anything from Stephen yet?' she asked.

'Probably a bit early,' replied Sam, shrugging on his jacket. 'I'll give him a call in a while if we still haven't heard. He did say he might pop over with Laura today anyway, now that the marquee's here. She needs to measure up, apparently. Besides there are no guarantees that the police's stance will change, even with Laura's further statement. Granted they're viewing Giles's visit to the hospital as suspicious, but they still need something more concrete to go on before they can act. We just have to hope that they do decide to investigate further; taking a look at Giles's car will be the crucial thing.'

'Laura must feel happier about things though, surely? At the very least the police seem to be taking her more seriously, and rightly so, it's a big thing for her.'

Sam regarded her squarely as he zipped up his jacket. 'Hmm, although the potential repercussions worry me somewhat. She's still very vulnerable.'

Freya stopped in her tracks. 'What do you mean repercussions?' she asked, looking up.

'Well, think about it for a minute. Laura's husband died five years ago and yet, according to Laura, Francis Drummond still takes every opportunity he can to make fun of her or threaten her even. Doesn't that strike you as odd? I mean, why bother, after all this time?'

'Because he likes to throw his weight around. He's a bully, you know that.'

'He is,' continued Sam, 'but bullies usually have something to gain by their behaviour. Often they're cowards, or vulnerable themselves, using their actions to hide the truth from the world.

It's almost as if he needs to keep Laura under control, subdued, if you like. But what do you suppose would make him want to do that? What possible threat could Laura pose to him?'

Freya's eyes widened. 'You're scaring me now, Sam. Are you saying you think Laura's in danger of some sort?'

'No, I think that's a tad melodramatic, but it does make me curious. And now that she's made an accusation against Francis's son, which looks as if it might stick, I don't suppose he'll be feeling particularly charitable towards her.'

'Then we should say something to Laura, warn her.'

Sam took her arm gently. 'I think Stephen has it pretty much covered,' he said with meaning, giving Freya a long look.

She stared back at him. 'You've discussed this with him, haven't you?' she accused. 'That's what you were talking about for ages on the phone yesterday; nothing to do with the wedding at all.'

'It was mentioned, yes, but don't go getting on your high horse about all this . . .' He gave her a small smile. 'Stephen really is the best person to deal with this as far as Laura's concerned. I'd say he's got to know her pretty well over the last few days . . .'

Freya opened her mouth to speak again, but Sam dropped her arm, and turned for the door.

'And not the way you're thinking either, so you can take that look off your face. I've honestly never seen Stephen behave this way before, about anybody. He obviously cares about Laura a great deal, and I think he deserves some respect, or at the very least, our trust.'

With that he walked out into the yard, leaving Freya staring after him in astonishment, a small smile gathering at the corners of her mouth. Well, well, well. Now that was something she'd never expected to hear. Stephen might be acting out of character, but he wasn't the only one. In all the years she'd known Sam, she'd never heard him stick up for his brother like that before. Times certainly were a changing. She hurried through the door, pulling it firmly shut behind her.

★ ★ ★

Laura could hardly contain her excitement. At least she thought it was excitement. The bubbling, fizzing feeling in her stomach might well be sheer terror, she acknowledged. She gazed around her at the huge open space, at the multitude of tables and chairs that filled the marquee, and took a very deep breath. Then she closed her eyes.

She stayed that way for several minutes, letting images fill her mind, mentally roaming the hedgerows, seeking out the colours and the textures that would bring the pictures in her head to life. The tables, the great arch of the marquee entrance, the tented ceiling, all of it was a blank canvas waiting to be filled. When she opened her eyes, she gave a nod of satisfaction. She had several days of hard graft ahead of her, but it was going to look beautiful, more beautiful than anything she had ever created in her life before. And the thought brought a sudden rush of tears to her eyes.

She glanced at her watch to confirm that she didn't have the luxury of any more time here and, whilst it would have been nice to make some sketches, or measure one or two things, Laura knew that it wasn't really necessary, not for her. Her designs weren't that structured; they were organic, they grew out of themselves, and however hard she tried to think things through in advance, she knew that in practice she rarely looked at any plans she had made. Instead, she sat down with her raw materials heaped around her and let the strange alchemy begin. It made her fingers twitch just thinking about it.

With one final glance about her, Laura strode from the marquee. Stephen had disappeared almost the minute they got here, saying that he would only be in the way and she should have some time on her own to think about things without his interference. More like gone in search of a bacon butty she reckoned, but she couldn't begrudge him that. He had offered to help her today, and having done a recce on the church first thing this morning, now she needed to plunder what the fields and hedgerows had to offer, and that was going to take some time, and manpower.

She finally rooted him out in the kitchen, having a bit of a heart to heart with Sam by the look of things, but he jumped up the minute he saw her.

He turned to her and smiled. 'Are we sorted?' he asked, stretching out his back and giving his neck a flex.

'We are, although are you sure you're up for this? We're going to walk miles this afternoon.'

Stephen merely shrugged. 'Don't be fooled by appearances. I'll have you know this body is a finely tuned machine.'

Laura caught Sam's eye and winked. 'We'll see,' she said. 'Come on then, no time for dallying. It's a mile-and-a-half to the first place we need to go.'

'Not that I'm wimping out or anything,

but you do realise there's a perfectly good car outside?'

She grinned. 'Perhaps I should rephrase that last statement. It's a four-mile drive to the nearest place you can park, and then a mile-and-a-half walk across the fields.'

Stephen looked back at Sam, and she didn't catch what he said next, but judging by the expression on his face when he turned back to her, she could guess.

★ ★ ★

It had been a shrewd investment buying Clarence Cottage all those years ago. Back then, she'd been an accounts clerk, and neither she nor David could have foreseen the direction her 'career' would take. They had fallen in love with the cottage primarily because of its cosy charm but, whilst they appreciated that it also had a large garden and outbuildings, they hadn't thought much beyond them at the time. Now, these sheds were filled with tables and, looking around her

197

in the dimming light, Laura was grateful indeed. Their afternoon's work was heaped before them.

Every surface groaned with an array of greenery, fruits, grasses and grains, with hues of every colour ranging from vibrant oranges and reds, to dusky pinks and purples, lime greens, soft greens, and warming ochres.

Her hair was tangled with straw and cobwebs, her skin flushed by the sun and wind, and her fingers stained with sap and juice, but Laura felt profoundly at peace. She was knackered, but filled with an immense satisfaction, something she had not felt in a long time. She sat on a wooden chair beside one of the tables and smiled to herself. Usually, the fields and hedgerows were hers alone; she might see the odd rider or dog walker, but invariably her day was spent in solitude. This afternoon she had shared her knowledge with someone else. Where she'd walked, Stephen walked, out of necessity saying little, but at times stopping to ask her questions, and listening to her enthusiastic responses with a keen ear and a ready smile. He had followed her instructions for what to pick and how to pick it to the letter, and had worked solidly without complaint. His company had been easy, familiar even, and reluctant though Laura had been to admit it, she had enjoyed the afternoon far more because of it. When he dropped her home, his kiss to her cheek had been soft, nothing more, but the memory of it now, still brought a renewed flush to her cheeks. She shook her head in wonder at the changes she could feel within herself. Who would have thought that Stephen Henderson of all people would be the person to bring that about?

She glanced outside at the rapidly falling night and began to scoop up sheaves of tawny foliage from one of the tables. They would need to be steeped in a glycerine solution to preserve their colour and pliability, and the sooner she did it, the better the result would be.

The back door to the cottage was still open, the light from the kitchen spilling a welcome square onto the path which led up the garden. She was only a few feet from the door when the first brilliant flash lit up the sky, followed quickly by another, then another. She flinched automatically, unable to see clearly for a few moments, but her feet carried her safely to the door. Once inside she threw the door closed, and hurriedly dumped her cargo on the table. Boris was right where she expected him to be, cowering up against the side of the Aga, his brown eyes ringed with white. She sank to the floor, wrapping her arms around his neck. Bonfire night was ages away yet, but every year the fireworks seemed to get earlier and earlier and, big dog he might be, but he was still terrified of the noise and bursts of light.

She remembered firework displays from her childhood, how her stomach had contracted with the thud of the rockets, noise that seemed to come from nowhere even though it was expected, the sharp staccato crackles leaving her ears ringing. Of course, now, for her, the fireworks had fallen silent, but she could recall the noisy confusion as if it was yesterday.

Another burst lit up the darkened room, the intensity of it making even Laura jump. She could feel the fur in Boris' throat quivering and knew that he was growling. Her murmured words of comfort were having little effect, and he broke free from her hold, running at the window, jumping. She would like to give whoever was being so irresponsible a piece of her mind, but there was little point; she would never be heard. The flashes were coming almost continually now, until, blinded, Laura could scarcely make out the room in front of her. Boris was frantic, running up and down the room, and out into the hallway. She realised belatedly that the light which alerted her to a caller at the front door was flashing too, and it was then that the first slivers of fear began to replace her anger.

She got to her feet, trying to catch hold of Boris, but he was lunging at the window and she was almost knocked over by his huge size. He was trying to protect her, she knew that, but the dog was clearly terrified too. Her own heart was hammering in her chest, and it gave a wild leap as a masked face appeared at the window, illuminated for a second by the flare outside. Whoever was outside was in her garden! And then, as an icy trail snaked down her back, everything began to make sense. This was not kids having irresponsible fun, nor was it an early bonfire party. This was a deliberate attack on her.

Laura grabbed hold of Boris' collar and dragged him across the floor and out into the hallway. She kicked the kitchen door closed, whimpering, and came to rest in the corner of the hallway, her back against the wall, her arms trying to contain the terrified dog. It was at least darker in the hallway, with the doors closed and no windows to broadcast the light from the fireworks. The door-bell alarm was still flashing, but the light from it was nothing compared with the onslaught in the kitchen. She could only imagine the noise level, and knew this was what was making Boris so scared, and her so panicked. She also realised that it was preventing her from thinking straight.

She closed her eyes and tried to concentrate for a moment, weighing up what she could do. There was no way she could go outside. Apart from being terrified, without fully functioning senses she would be defenceless; and Boris, despite his size, was a gentle dog and not given to aggressive behaviour. And then it hit her; the cold truth was that whoever was behind this definitely knew her, and knew the best way to scare her too. She clung to Boris even tighter, knowing that she was trapped in her own home until whoever was outside had finished intimidating her. Only then might she be able to venture back into the kitchen and root out her mobile. She was beginning to feel slightly more in control when she suddenly realised that she had no memory of locking her back door. Granted, she normally did it automatically when she had finished outside for the day, but in her earlier haste she couldn't remember whether she had or not. The thought made her stomach leap in shock; they could be in her kitchen right now . . .

To her surprise, this new fear brought anger rushing to the surface. How dare they corner her in her own home? Cowardly bullies, she thought, that's all they were, and it was about time she stood up for herself. She flung open the door to the kitchen, realising a split second too late that the room was now pitch black. She cannoned straight into a hard body on the other side of the door, the shock causing her legs to buckle alarmingly. She felt a cry loose itself from her lips, and a pair of arms caught hold of her as she dropped; strong arms which held her up and then held her close. She breathed in a scent that had become so familiar over the last few days, and this time instead of evading Stephen's touch, she returned it, letting his solid warmth seep into her.

The tears came as she felt his hand move to cradle her head. She could feel his lips moving against her hair, saying words she could neither hear nor see, yet words her heart imagined. They clung together silently in the dark for several moments until Laura felt a sudden need to see his face, to talk, and to understand. Slowly, she disentangled herself and doubled back to flick on the light switch, flinching once more as the kitchen sprang into relief.

Stephen's face was dark with anger, but his eyes were soft on hers.

'They've gone,' he said. 'It's okay.'

He bent down, stretching out one hand in front of him, and as Laura watched, Boris slunk across the floor, half his usual height, his tail tucked between his legs, but with just the faintest twitch of a wag. He pushed his nose into Stephen's palm, his body quivering gently, from fear still, or a sense of delight, Laura couldn't tell. He sat on the floor pulling Laura down too and held the dog in a jumble of limbs between them. 'Who were they?' she whispered.

'I've no idea,' Stephen replied. 'Three of them, all wearing masks. It's a wonder they didn't kill themselves, letting off fireworks at such close range, but I imagine that when the police catch up with them, they'll be easy to spot; their clothes must be covered in burns, and stink too I shouldn't wonder.'

Laura nodded. 'And will the police catch up with them?' she asked.

'If they've anything about them, they will. Particularly as I told them a good place to start looking.'

She swallowed. 'You reckon it was Giles then?'

'Not personally. He's far too cowardly for that,' sneered Stephen, 'but he'll have found some thugs for hire. His sort generally do.'

'I can't believe he'd be so stupid. I mean he's now being investigated for a hit and run, right? How does this possibly make things any better for him?'

Stephen sighed. 'Well, he might be loaded, and he might think the world is his to command, but that doesn't mean he isn't thick as shit. Whereas you and I might approach a difficulty with rational thought and integrity, I suspect that when the Drummond family are faced with a problem, they simply require it to be got rid of; I don't suppose they're especially bothered about how.' Stephen sank his hands into the dog's fur. 'And of course there is another way to look at it . . .'

'Which is?'

'That by scaring you senseless, you might change your mind about what you saw on the day of the accident . . . that you might even retract your statement, telling the police that you simply got it wrong . . .'

'But that's ridiculous!'

'It's not actually . . . Because today they only scared you. They lit fireworks, knowing that the noise would terrify Boris and that the flashes and flares would disorientate you. By taking out Boris, it effectively made you very vulnerable, which is just what they wanted of course —'

'Yes, but . . .'

Stephen held up his hand. 'And if they could do that today . . . what might they get up to the next day, or the next . . .'

Laura stared at the gentle expression on Stephen's face. He couldn't possibly mean that, he was just being melodramatic; but the more she looked at him, the more she could see the truth in what he had said. A shiver ran through her. Despite all that had happened to her in the past, Laura still believed in a world that was kind and good. Things like this only happened in soap operas, not real life. And yet, it had happened. Giles Drummond had knocked down a defenceless old lady and driven away; left her for dead at the side of the road, and even now, when faced with the possibility of having to accept responsibility for his actions, he was trying to wheedle his way out of it. People did do bad things, she had seen the proof of it, and Stephen was right. She felt his hand cover hers.

'I'm not trying to scare you, Laura, but

we need to think carefully about what we do next. I'm worried about you being on your own, and I know you're very capable, and independent . . .' he gave a wry smile, 'and you'll probably punch me for coming over all macho on you, but even though I know all this, I'm still not happy about you being by yourself. I don't want to point out the obvious for risk of permanent injury to my nether regions, but where Giles is concerned your deafness puts you at a real disadvantage, and he knows it.'

A few months ago, she would have been angry at Stephen's words, and his nether regions would most definitely have been under threat, but today, she simply smiled. She *had* changed over the last few weeks, and however much she wanted to dispute that fact, her current feelings were proof, and they would have to be faced up to very soon. She wasn't at all sure what she wanted to do about them, but for now at least the thought of Stephen not leaving her alone was stomach churningly lovely. A warm glow

209

began to rise up from her toes.

'So what do we do now?' she asked, blushing.

'Well, our most pressing business is still Freya and Sam's wedding, and nothing must prevent that from being the glorious day it deserves to be, which also includes giving your decorations the chance to shine, by the way. As all your materials are here, and you're going to need help gathering more of them and transporting them too, I suggest that I bagsy your spare room . . . just for a few days until we see how things lie. That way I can help make sure that the wedding arrangements go according to plan, and I can be on hand in case there's any repeat of this evening. I dread to think what might have happened if I hadn't been around.'

Laura hardly dared to think what colour her face might be, but apart from that she suddenly realised what had been flitting about in her brain over the last few minutes.

'I was wondering about that,' she

said. 'Don't think that I'm not stupidly grateful of course, but why are you here? I thought we'd said goodbye for the evening.'

'Ah . . .' Stephen smiled, patting his stomach. 'I'd like to say something worthy and heroic, but sadly it was a case of having got home, realising that I was knackered, starving, and couldn't face cooking, and wondering if maybe you felt the same? I was going to suggest a takeaway. The Indian place at the far end of the High Street is very good, it does home delivery too.'

The look on Stephen's face was priceless. 'Well, it's honest at least.' She grinned. 'And . . . actually not a bad idea. Now that I've thought about it, I'm starving as well. I could murder a good curry.'

She ruffled Boris's fur one more time and, laughing, struggled to get to her feet. Stephen followed suit until they stood rather shyly in the middle of the room.

'What about my other suggestion?'

211

began Stephen, scuffing at the floor with his foot. 'Do you think perhaps I should stay for a bit?'

'Let's get some food sorted first,' she replied, 'then we can talk about it. I'll see if I can find a menu.'

She turned away so that Stephen wouldn't see her smile. She didn't want him to think she was a complete pushover.

14

Stephen was not normally given to strong emotions, nor had he found it easy in the past to show them, but as Freya moved slowly down the aisle towards him, his throat constricted almost painfully. Beside him, Sam stood waiting patiently for his bride, and as she neared, Stephen's heart swelled with delight and pride.

Freya looked radiant, and more than that, thought Stephen, she was totally and utterly, blissfully in love. It shone out of her, in the way she walked, the way her eyes sparkled as she met those of the people sitting in the pews she passed, and the way she clasped her bouquet excitedly in front of her, a beautiful tribute to the life she had made with Sam, and one which they would now share forever.

Rosy apples jostled for space with huge deep pink peonies; eucalyptus leaves and sage sat between glowing hips and golden pears; pale roses met with dark dusky blackberries and huge speckled poppy heads. If Stephen hadn't helped collect all these beautiful things he would never have believed it for himself, and two rows behind him, Laura sat in the church, where he hoped she was also bursting with pride at her achievement. He had heard the gasps of astonishment from the congregation as they filed into the church, and it hurt him more than anything to know that she could not hear them herself. But she must surely see the delight on the faces, the fingers that pointed out her stunning decorations where the unusual and the traditional sat side by side in such perfect harmony.

A golden beam of afternoon sun filtered through the huge windows in front of him and warmed the stone flags onto which Freya now stepped. The light settled upon her and Sam and, as the vicar came forward to join them both in marriage, a wide smile settled over Stephen's face. He had come a long way since the days when he had fought Sam every step of the way; fought even to take Freya from him, and had she not come to her senses when she did, they would both have been condemned to an unhappy future. It had taken a long time for things to come right again, for Stephen even longer than Freya and Sam, but as he watched the couple in front of him now, he realised that things were just as they should be.

* * *

It was only a matter of hours since he and Laura had last left the marquee. They had worked into the wee small hours, dressing and pinning, arranging and perfecting, but now, as the wedding guests filed in to take their places, he increased his pressure on Laura's hand. The space looked amazing, and the expression on her face was mirrored by his own; a mixture of excitement, of childlike wonder, and an overwhelming relief that it did indeed look as good as they had imagined it would. Appleyard

Farm was shining like a jewel today, and the woman by his side had been responsible for most of it.

The conversation was increasing to a steady hum, and Stephen knew that this was when Laura would feel most ill at ease. It was hard enough for her to follow what people were saying in a crowd, but when they were eating and drinking as well, it unwittingly made their speech almost impossible for her to decipher. For the most part, he could do nothing but stay by her side and make sure that she could at least understand his words. Beyond that he had one or two little surprises up his sleeve, which he hoped would be received in the spirit in which they were offered.

He almost hadn't told Sam and Freya what he had done, fearing they would laugh at him, or even be angry with him for making arrangements for their wedding day without their knowledge. But the fact that Freya had turned away when he told them, on the pretext of putting the kettle on, had meant more to him than her words ever could. He had seen the tears welling in her eyes, and although he knew he still had much to prove to her about his behaviour, her reaction was more than he could have wished for. He also had her and Sam's blessing which made everything all the easier of course. His speech nestled in his jacket pocket and he patted it for the umpteenth time that day. He almost knew it off by heart but automatically felt for it just the same.

He had arranged for Laura to sit at the top table, alongside him, and with Freya's best friend, Merry, who had acted as maid of honour, on her other side. He knew that Merry had owned a florist shop once upon a time and hoped that the two of them would have plenty to talk about. As they took their seats, he caught the eye of one of the guests sitting directly on the table opposite and gave a nervous smile. His stomach was in knots.

★ ★ ★

Laura concentrated on her food for a moment. The room was a confused jumble of words, gathered here and there as she looked out onto the sea of faces in front of her, but to her surprise she was still enjoying herself. It didn't much matter that she couldn't follow what people were saying all the time, because everywhere she looked, she saw smiling faces and the mood was infectious. Most eyes were quite rightly on Freya, but she saw many looking at her huge urns filled with the countryside, and bounty from the farm, and the smiles remained in place. She even caught the eye of a few people, folk she had known for years, only this time instead of looking away, or worse, pretending they hadn't seen her, they held her look, nodded and smiled. Something subtle had changed in their reactions, and with a jolt she realised that she was the reason.

Previously, her gaze had been a challenge, a dare to prove her suspicions right, and an opportunity to justify her own poor behaviour. She realised now

that she had made people uncomfortable, embarrassed even, and had deserved
the responses she got, simply because
she had given people no other choice. A
scowl was met with a scowl, just as now, a
smile was met with a smile. It was a simple equation, but one which had taken
her far too long to work out.

She realised that Stephen was talking
to her again, and leaned in towards him.
He had, as he suggested, moved into
her spare bedroom and, whether it was
the sight of his car, a constant compan-
ion to hers on the driveway, or the fact
that he insisted they sit with the curtains
open every evening in case anyone happened to glance in and see that she was
not alone, she wasn't sure, but nothing
untoward had happened since the incident with the fireworks. In fact, nothing
untoward had happened at all, and
Laura wasn't entirely sure if she was dis-
appointed or not. They had got on well
after the initial embarrassment of finding themselves sleeping under the same
roof; beyond that their relationship had

been friendly and companionable, but nothing more.

Now he seemed a little jittery, and she hoped it was simply nerves at the thought of his looming speech. Throughout the day he had been attentiveness personified, making sure that she was okay, that she wasn't too nervous herself, or feeling uncomfortable. At times, he had seemed to want to say something more than the words that had actually come out of his mouth, but the feeling passed again, and Laura was left wondering. As she looked at him now, she realised that she was not concentrating at all on what he was saying, but instead focusing on the full curve of his mouth, the slight dimple that appeared in his right cheek when he spoke, and the warmth in his eyes. She frowned and asked him to repeat what he had said.

'I'm sorry, I was miles away,' she added. And she was. She was thinking very much about kissing him.

She almost missed the start of Stephen's speech. She was deep in conversation with Merry, who was fascinated to know more about her business, and it was only when she stopped talking and touched Laura's arm, that she realised Stephen was tapping the side of his glass with a knife. She straightened up, and arranged her face into a polite smile. She would have to take her cue from the other wedding guests about when to laugh as she doubted very much that she would be able to follow what he was saying from this angle.

To her surprise, a tall, very elegant lady directly opposite her got to her feet and fixed Laura with a beaming smile. She was even more surprised when she signed *Hello, I'm Natalie*.

Tentatively, she signed back. Natalie smiled again, and then looked to Stephen, giving him a nod. There was a momentary pause and then her hands began to fly as Stephen started to speak.

'Well, this is a first for me,' she began to sign, 'and so before I launch into what might yet turn out to be the worst best man's speech you've ever heard, I'm going to ask you all to be patient with me. I know that most of you here are well aware of the gory details of my past as far as Sam and Freya are concerned, and could be forgiven for wondering how on earth I've ended up giving a speech at their wedding . . . So, I'm also going to ask you to be lenient with me too as I try to explain how I think that's happened. Firstly, though, I'd like to welcome you all here today, and of course thank you for coming. I genuinely don't think there's a soul left in the village, but Appleyard Orchard has been at the centre of our community for a very long time, and I know it means the world to Freya and Sam to see you all here. Without further ado then, I'd like you to raise a glass in toast to the deliriously happy couple . . . Freya and Sam.'

Laura raised her glass with a grin, watching the stream of bubbles in her champagne rising to the surface and popping. It was much how her stomach felt. She waited for everyone's attention to switch back to Stephen, all the while never taking her eyes off Natalie, whose hands moved back into position.

'I'd also like to make an introduction before I go any further . . . Some of you may have noticed that my speech today is being signed, so I'd very much like you all to welcome Natalie. She is a British Sign Language tutor from Hereford, and has very kindly offered to give me a hand here today, quite literally . . . and at very short notice too. Thank you, Natalie.'

Natalie broke off to give a little wave, before continuing with her interpreting. 'Some of you might already have worked out that the reason why Natalie is here today is sitting on my left. For those of you who don't know, her name is Laura and she's profoundly deaf. More importantly, she's responsible for today's stunning floral decorations, and as I'm just about to say some incredibly nice things about her, I thought she should be able to 'hear' them.'

Laura risked a tiny peep to her right, knowing that Stephen would be looking at her. She didn't want to blush bright red in front of all these people, but then would that really be such a big price to pay considering what Stephen had done for her? Her eyes met his, surprised to see that he was blushing too.

'When Sam first asked me to be his best man, I'll admit I was a little surprised; but I realised very quickly how humbled I was at being asked, and how generous Sam was being in asking me. That's just like Sam. He's always seen the good in me, even when we were young, and I spent most of my time being jealous of him and consequently trying to make his life as miserable as possible. For a long time, I pretty much succeeded, but a year or so ago, all that began to change when a very special person came back into Sam's life. That person was, of course, Freya. I think they first got engaged in primary school, and even then, it was clear that the universe had decreed they should be together. Despite my best efforts to keep them apart, fate intervened and brought them back together again, fortunately for me.

'I say fortunately because from the moment they did, it gave Freya the perfect opportunity to let me know in no uncertain terms what she thought of me, urging me to grow up and to start taking responsibility for myself. Much to my surprise, I listened. It hasn't always been easy, and I dare say I still get things wrong, but Sam and Freya are the kind of people who go the extra mile for anyone, even me, and that's really why I'm standing here today.

'I'll also admit that I didn't really get it, this whole love thing. I could see how much Sam and Freya were in love, but I never understood what that meant, what that felt like, or, perhaps more importantly, why I didn't or couldn't feel the same. It wasn't until recently when I quite literally got knocked for six that I began to feel these alien emotions. It's possible that the blow to the head I sustained might be the cause, but I'd be willing to bet it had a lot more to do with a beautiful young lady who came into my life very suddenly one afternoon, and since then, in my head at least, has refused to leave.'

Natalie broke off her signing, looking rather puzzled. She exchanged a look with Laura and gave a slight shrug as if in apology. Clearly, Stephen had stopped speaking for some reason and, as Laura leaned forward to see what the problem was, Stephen turned to look squarely at her.

'You're going to kill me,' he said with a grin.

Laura, whose heart was suddenly beating very fast, was still trying to process the rush of emotions that Stephen's words had already created when he continued to speak.

'Because I'm about to tell everyone here that I love you . . .'

Laura looked up in astonishment to see Natalie signing *Oh My God . . .*

Stephen began again. 'Laura has a huge soul, is kind and incredibly brave, but sadly, and for reasons best known to themselves, certain people have tried to break her spirit over the years, and she has been on her own for far too long. She has taught me a great deal, about myself, however, about what makes me happy, and what it is to share the life of another. I find myself being nice, and considerate, compassionate even, and believe me these are things that never came easily before. I think of her before myself, in fact I think of her all the time, and it's only now that I realise what it means to love someone else . . . So, as I say my closing words, in celebration of the love that Freya and Sam share, and with hope that it continues undiminished, you can be sure that I mean what I say, because, to both my surprise and yours, I finally get what this thing called love is all about. To Freya and Sam.'

Laura imagined that the noise in the room at this point must be deafening. She could see glasses being raised, mouths open in surprise, repeating Stephen's toast, whooping and calling, and hands crashing together, clapping feverishly. What would it be like if she could hear it all? It was hard enough trying to think inside a ball of silence, her brain frantically attempting to recall Stephen's words in case she'd got them wrong, but the look on his face seemed to suggest she had not. She looked over at Natalie, who was nodding and smiling from ear to ear, then back again to Stephen who wore a curious expression, almost as if he was waiting for a punch to land, but then as her mouth began to curve upwards, following the trajectory her heart was also taking, she saw his expression begin to mirror her own. The last thing she saw as he bent to kiss her was Freya, grinning like a loon over his shoulder.

15

Stephen looked down at the piece of paper he was still clutching and dropped it on the table. It was the speech he had so carefully written and rehearsed and then completely ignored. He still wasn't sure what had made him do it, except that as he began to speak about Freya and Sam, he had suddenly realised how very simple things were when you loved someone, how very 'right' things could feel, and for a split second, had been utterly terrified that this might change. Without really thinking about where they were, telling Laura that he loved her had suddenly been the most important thing in the world.

Freya and Merry had immediately whisked Laura away, and they were now standing in a huddle, broad grins on their faces, hands flapping in their excitement. The memory of his first kiss with Laura still tingled on his lips, and if the shy but meaningful glances she kept giving him were anything to go by, he wouldn't have to wait too long for another.

Beside him, Sam refilled his glass.

'Get that down you,' he said, giving Stephen's arm a nudge. He took a swallow from his own glass. 'What an absolutely bloody amazingly stupendous day,' he added.

Stephen who, bizarrely, was now finding words difficult could only grin in reply, but he took a large glug of champagne anyway.

'Who would have thought it?' mused Sam. 'My brother finally becoming an adult, after all these years.'

'Don't be so cruel,' he said in reply. 'I'm still in a state of shock myself.' But he smiled at his brother, recognising the truth in his words.

'Actually, mate,' said Sam. 'I'm proud of you. Proud of what you've done too. I see now that you had an ulterior motive, but all this business with Drummond can't have been easy. Laura would never have had the courage to come forward as a witness to the hit and run if it wasn't for you, and now it actually looks as if that scumbag low-life is going to get his comeuppance. Have you heard any more?'

Stephen shook his head. 'Only what the police told me this morning; that they've impounded Giles' car pending an examination. They were very interested to hear of the incident with the fireworks the other night, and I have to say it's not looking good for Drummond.' He took another sip of his champagne, his eyes now firmly on Laura. 'I know none of this is over yet. It could rumble on for months; we might both have to give evidence, but all Laura ever wanted was for people to take her seriously, because of what's right, not because of some stupid grudge against the Drummond family . . . although God knows she'd have cause enough for that after the way they've treated her.'

'They're a powerful family; it's not easy standing up to bullies like that.'

'No . . . and I hope in time the villagers

come to see the truth of it too. Francis has employed a good many of them over the years, but I think now, more and more folk might start asking questions, and come forward in support of Laura and her allegations over David's death.'

Sam nodded grimly. 'I'm sure they will,' he replied. 'Which is of course the very thing Francis was seeking to avoid. Anyway, let's not think about that now. The DJ is giving me the eye, I think it might be time for me and my wife to have our first dance.'

'Sounds good that, me and my wife,' replied Stephen, grinning at his brother.

'It sure does!' Sam winked.

★ ★ ★

'But I can't dance!' protested Laura, laughing. 'Trust me, it's not a pretty sight.'

'Well, I don't believe that for one minute. Anyway, this is different.'

Laura studied Stephen's face. 'It's a disco, people will be dancing. How can it possibly be different?'

He took hold of her hand. 'Come on, I'll show you.'

Before she had a chance to protest any further, Laura found herself propelled through an archway into a smaller marquee which was sitting just behind the first. The space was dim apart from shimmering rays of silver light which flitted around the room courtesy of a series of disco balls which hung from the tented ceiling. Inside, just as she suspected, people were dancing. She slowed her movement, feeling the tug against Stephen's hand as she ground to a halt. He turned to look at her, his face lit by an excited grin.

'It'll be fine. Come on, I promise you.'

'I can't, Stephen, I'll make a complete prat of myself.'

He angled his head at her. 'Or no one will notice what you're doing at all . . .' He moved a little closer. 'Watch for a second, and tell me what you see.'

She looked at him quizzically.

'I know, it sounds stupid. But honestly,

just stand and watch . . .' He moved to stand a little behind her, pulling her into him, enfolding her in his arms. She leaned back into his warmth.

Her first, cursory glance, showed her nothing new; it was simply a room full of people who were dancing and laughing, moving their bodies in time with the music, just like she had done once upon a time. But then, as she watched, she began to pick out the details of what was happening. Two young girls were giggling madly, almost jumping with energy, their arms flailing above their heads. Next to them a middle-aged couple swayed together, her head on his shoulder, shuffling in the manner of every slow dance she had ever seen. She stared around the room, not understanding what she was looking at. How could some people be dancing to a slow record and yet others be leaping around?

A group of people moved past her, crossing slightly to the right where a chap standing behind a table smiled a greeting at them. He handed them what looked like a pair of headphones from a pile in front of him; bright purple and blue in colour, and when Laura looked back to the dance floor, she realised that everyone was wearing a pair.

She wriggled round in Stephen's arms until she was facing him again. 'What's going on? Why does everyone need headphones?' 'Because it's a silent disco. The headphones play the music, but without them on, no one can hear it in the room.' Laura thought for a moment. 'But what's the point in that?' Stephen brushed a curl of hair from out of her eye. 'Well, the headphones don't play the same music to everyone. They work by picking up wireless signals from the DJ's box of tricks, and he's broadcasting four different signals, which is why, if you look around the room, it looks a bit odd . . . People are dancing to different things.'

Laura turned to face the room for a moment and then back again. 'I still don't get it,' she said, frowning. Stephen dropped a kiss on the end of her nose.

'Well, if no one else can hear what you're listening to, does it matter how you dance . . . ?' It took a moment for the meaning of his words to penetrate her brain, but when they did, a slow smile began to spread across Laura's face. 'Oh my God, that's bloody brilliant, come on!' By the time they reached the centre of the floor, Laura was grinning from ear to ear. 'What shall we dance to?' she urged. 'I don't mind,' replied Stephen, 'I'll follow your lead.' 'Well, there is one song I remember dancing to when I was young — 'Wake Me Up Before You Go Go', by Wham. What do you think?' 'How about we go on three?' grinned Stephen, holding up three fingers. 'Three . . . two . . . one . . . Go!'

Laura felt the song flow through her mind, trying to move how she used to, letting the feel of it surge through her body, it had been such a long time . . . She closed her eyes and let herself go. A wild excitement began to fill her as her body became alive again, and after a few minutes, she opened her eyes risking a peep at Stephen. He looked a little self-conscious but nonetheless was moving in time to the music playing in his own head.

'Oh God, this is so silly!' Laura laughed. 'But it's the most fun I've had in . . . well, I can't remember when.'

Stephen started to answer, but clearly found that the combination of moving his arms and legs, trying to listen to imaginary music playing in his head, and speaking all at the same time was simply too much. He gave a series of odd movements as he tried to pick up the beat again, and then ground to a halt, laughing at himself.

The sight of him was too much for Laura. She collapsed in a fit of giggles that only got worse, the more she tried to stop them. She leaned against him, holding on for support, shaking with laughter and clutching onto her stomach which was beginning to hurt from the effort. It was some moments before she could speak again.

'I'm so sorry,' she spluttered helplessly.

'I shouldn't be laughing, but that was the funniest thing I've ever seen!'

'Perhaps I should wear the headphones after all; coordination has never been my strong point.' He looked at her then, a more serious expression on his face. 'Only trouble is, if I do that, I won't be able to dance with you or hear what you say.' He caught both her hands in his. 'Would you teach me how to sign, Laura? I mean it. And not just hello and goodbye, all of it. I want to be able to talk to you anywhere, and anytime, all the time.'

She leaned forward and kissed him gently, her body now up against his. 'I will,' she whispered, 'I promise.' She lay her head against his chest for a moment, before suddenly pulling away.

'You did this for me,' she said, her eyes wide, 'didn't you? I've only just realised.'

Stephen looked into her eyes, a soft expression on his face. 'Guilty as charged,' he said. 'I wanted you to have something today that was on your terms, something that wouldn't make you feel out of place, or different to everyone else. To be honest, when I booked the disco I wasn't planning on hijacking my best man's speech and declaring my feelings for you . . . but I had sort of hoped this might do it . . .' he trailed off.

'No one's ever done anything like this for me before,' whispered Laura, reaching up to touch the side of his face.

'Yeah, they have,' countered Stephen. 'A while ago maybe, but I'm sure they have.'

Laura studied his face. 'Perhaps,' she said. 'A long time ago.' She looked around, at a room full of people, all of whom smiled at her when she caught their eye. A few months ago, simply being here would have filled her with dread, but now it filled her with hope. Freya and Sam were off to one side, as were Merry and her husband. She could feel her past receding into the distance as if she no longer had need of it. Her future was beckoning instead.

She turned back to Stephen. 'I think I can hear a slow dance starting,' she said.

'So maybe now would be the right time to start your first lesson in sign language.' She pulled away slightly to make a sign with her hands, speaking the words at the same time. She touched a finger to his lips. 'No talking now,' she said.

'That was one of the very first signs I learned,' laughed Stephen. 'Call me forward, but that's one you won't need to teach me.' And he held her gaze with eyes that sparkled with emotion as he signed back the words *I love you*.

A Letter from Emma

Hello, and thank you so much for choosing to read this book. I hope you enjoyed reading these stories as much as I enjoyed writing them. So if you'd like to stay updated on what's coming next, please do sign up to my newsletter here and you'll be the first to know!

www.bookouture.com/emma-davies

Merry Mistletoe, *Spring Fever*, *Gooseberry Fool* and *Blackberry Way* make up the series of *A Year at Appleyard Farm*, and they're particularly special to me, not least of all because it's in the first of these books, *Merry Mistletoe*, that we first meet my favourite character of all time, Amos Fry. In fact, I fell in love with him so much that I always knew that one day

I would have to write his story and share it with the world. I never really knew what it was, but last year, when I had my idea for my summer book, *The Beekeeper's Cottage*, I finally got my chance and Amos's story was told. And I think I did him proud.

But these books are also special because they were written when my writing career was in its infancy. I had just got my first publishing deal with Letting In Light when I suddenly had an idea for a seasonal novella which became *Merry Mistletoe*. It was, however, never intended to become part of a series, but it was so popular that I was soon thinking about what could come next. I have a real passion for rural crafts and settings which evoke our glorious countryside, and so when I began to think about the next book, it made sense to set it in the spring time to take advantage of this. Summer and autumn soon followed.

Having folks take the time to get in touch really does make my day, and if you'd like to contact me, then I'd love to hear from you. The easiest way to do this is by finding me on Twitter and Facebook, or you could also pop by my website where you can read about my love of Pringles among other things . . .

I hope to see you again very soon, and in the meantime, if you've enjoyed your visit to Appleyard Farm, I would really appreciate a few minutes of your time to leave a review or post on social media. Every single review makes a massive difference and is very much appreciated!

Until next time,

Love, Emma xx

We do hope that you have enjoyed reading this large print book.

Did you know that all of our titles are available for purchase?

We publish a wide range of high quality large print books including:
Romances, Mysteries, Classics
General Fiction
Non Fiction and Westerns

Special interest titles available in large print are:
The Little Oxford Dictionary
Music Book, Song Book
Hymn Book, Service Book

Also available from us courtesy of Oxford University Press:
Young Readers' Dictionary
(large print edition)
Young Readers' Thesaurus
(large print edition)

For further information or a free brochure, please contact us at:
Ulverscroft Large Print Books Ltd.,
The Green, Bradgate Road, Anstey,
Leicester, LE7 7FU, England.
Tel: (00 44) 0116 236 4325
Fax: (00 44) 0116 234 0205

Other titles in the
Linford Romance Library:

THE SUMMER OF LOVE

John Darley

The sixties are swinging – but not so much for young fashion shop owner Joanie. All she needs is love, though it's not forthcoming where her mother is concerned. Only the aunt who Joanie lives with seems to care for her. Then she meets Martin, an airline pilot, who shows her love she can respond to – yet he's not all he appears to be. But then Joanie has her own secrets too. It will take a near-tragedy before matters are resolved . . .